SHERLOCK HOLMES

AND

THE LONDON PARTICULAR

[Being another manuscript found in the dispatch box of
Dr. John H. Watson
In the vault of Cox & Co., Charing Cross, London]

Book Five in the Series,
Sherlock Holmes and the American Literati

As Edited By

Daniel D. Victor, Ph.D.

Paperback ISBN 978-1-78705-420-2
ePub ISBN 978-1-78705-421-9
PDF ISBN 978-1-78705-422-6

MX Publishing
335 Princess Park Manor, Royal Drive,
London, N11 3GX
www.mxpublishing.com

Cover design by Brian Belanger

Also by Daniel D. Victor

The Seventh Bullet:
The Further Adventures of Sherlock Holmes

A Study in Synchronicity

The Final Page of Baker Street
(Book One in the series,
Sherlock Holmes and the American Literati)

Sherlock Holmes and the Baron of Brede Place
(Book Two in the series,
Sherlock Holmes and the American Literati)

Seventeen Minutes to Baker Street
(Book Three in the series,
Sherlock Holmes and the American Literati)

The Outrage at the Diogenes Club
(Book Four in the series,
Sherlock Holmes and the American Literati)

Sherlock Holmes and the Shadows of St Petersburg

3

Another for Norma, Seth and Ethan

Acknowledgements

Many thanks to Mark Holzband, Barry Smolin, Sandy Cohen, David Marcum, Judy Grabiner, Ethan Victor, Seth Victor, and Norma Silverman for their time, their suggestions, and their encouragement.

True London fog . . . reached maturity in the 1880s when its repeated visitations during the winter months caused widespread social anxiety and nervous concern about crime and disorder and inspired many writers to treat it as a looming presence, alive and malignant.

— Christine L. Corton
London Fog: The Biography

A Note on the Text

Footnotes followed by (JHW) were included by Dr. Watson in the original manuscript. Footnotes followed by (DDV) were, like the book's title and chapter headnotes, added by the editor.

Chapter One

In Medias Res

Upon sallying out this morning
encountered the old-fashioned pea soup London fog
— of a gamboge color. It was lifted, however, from the ground
& floated in mid-air. When lower, it is worse.
— Herman Melville
Journal of a Visit to
London and the Continent

i

A large rectangle of light exploded in the dense fog before us.

"What is it?" I cried out.

"An open door, Watson!" Sherlock Holmes exclaimed, his words muffled in the thick air. "Follow me," he said, pointing at the sudden illumination.

The sun had set hours before, and we had been feeling our way through the murk as best we could. What had begun as harmless wisps in the morning air had by late evening thickened into one of those impenetrable yellow fogs that used to roll down the streets of London during cold winter nights. Even now, some thirty years later, one finds it difficult to forget those smothering, all-encompassing shrouds — dense enough to cause the unfamiliar to lose their way at their very own thresholds, thick enough to rattle the most knowledgeable of pedestrians concerning their whereabouts.

"Through this gate!" Holmes commanded. "Whoever's inside should be able to fix our location."

Marking Holmes' voice and positioned only a few paces behind him and our new acquaintance — American journalist Richard Harding Davis — I inched forward. After a few more paces, I was close enough to see Holmes point out the pilaster to which the gate was hinged. One more step through the yellow mist and I could distinguish a brass plaque with the number eleven etched into its face. As good fortune would have it, the numeral heralded the very house we had been seeking.

Suddenly, a human silhouette filled the brightness; and an instant later the shadowy figure was rushing out the door. The dark shape ran past us toward the open gate, and I sensed more than saw a long, black coat and wide-brimmed hat.

"I say!" shouted Holmes, but the phantom had disappeared — safely concealed behind an oily curtain of fog.

With the muted tap of the American's walking stick indicating the way, I shuffled up the wide, black-asphalt path towards the light and proceeded to stumble over a trio of steps I had not seen. To make matters worse, I careened into a small but protruding wooden letter-box attached to the inside of the open door. It hung about a yard below the fanlight and bore a small brass lock on its lid. Even in the confusion created by the fog, I remember wondering as I followed Holmes and Davis inside, why an interior letter-box required locking.

ii

In contrast to the atmospheric gloom we had just escaped, everything within the entrance hall — the parquet floor, the burgundy-papered walls, the candle flames dancing wildly in their brass sconces — appeared especially sharp and crisp. I had to rub my eyes to regain my normal vision.

Sherlock Holmes, however, was already focusing his attention on an adjacent hallway.

"Hullo?" he called down the empty corridor.

Silence.

"Hullo?" he tried again.

Besides the lingering remains of the faintest of echoes, there was again no answer. Yet Holmes held up a cautious forefinger. "Listen," he said softly. "Do you hear it?"

Davis and I stood motionless, straining our ears for the slightest sound.

It took a moment, but then I did manage to discern a faint rasping — something like the heavy breathing one associates with deep sleep, and I pointed in the direction of the sitting room from where it seemed to come.

Holmes nodded and fixed Davis with a questioning stare. I recognised the look. It was designed to elicit from the American a final decision about moving forward or quitting the premises. After all, it was at Davis' request that we had braved the fog to come here in the first place.

In point of fact, we were seeking the mysterious woman who earlier that day had stolen a valuable diamond necklace from the American. Though its financial worth alone warranted its return, there was more to the piece than its monetary value. The necklace had been given to Davis for safe delivery to a mutual friend at the behest of the Queen.

Even with so distinguished a provenance, however, I wondered if Davis would dare trespass into a private house to negotiate the necklace's recovery. I had no doubt that Holmes and I were prepared to take the risk. For proof of our resolve, one need look no further than two years before when in search of the murderer of Cadogan West, the two of us had illegally entered the rooms of Hugo Oberstein, the notorious German agent.

About Davis' bravado I was much less confident. It was then only 1897. He had yet to perform those deeds of derring-do that would earn him the title of adventurous reporter. He had, for example, not yet involved himself in actual combat, as he would in Cuba when reporting the Spanish-American conflict — or faced down the prospects of a German firing squad when mistaken for a British spy as would occur years later at the start of the Great War. No, when we entered the house at No. 11 Boston Street that foggy night, we knew little about the pluck and mettle of Richard Harding Davis.

In retrospect, of course, the answer to Holmes' query should have been obvious. Presaging the daredevil Davis would become, the American responded with a quick nod; and my friend, having gained the encouragement he sought, led us through the hallway and into the brightly lit sitting room.

iii

Our attention immediately fell upon a grey-haired man in evening dress who sat collapsed on a red-plush couch before the remains of a fire in the hearth. Breathing loudly with his chin upon his chest, he might have been asleep or in some sort of stupor. Clearly, it was *his* snores that we had heard from the entry hall.

"Do you suppose he lives here?" I asked.

"He's the butler," Holmes observed. "Note the horizontal stripes of his waistcoat."

"And the out-dated cut of his suit," Davis was quick to add. Extending his stick, the American attempted to poke the inert butler into consciousness. "You there!" Davis commanded. "What's going on here? Where is everyone?"

In response, the man's eyelids fluttered open; his rheumy brown eyes rolled upward; and then, with the lids closing, his head lolled further down upon his waistcoat.

I leaned forward and smelt his foetid breath. "Drunk," I announced, wondering aloud why a servant in such a state had been allowed to occupy a place in the sitting room.

Holmes creased his brow; and the hollow silence in the rest of the house allowed an ominous feeling to take hold in each of us.

Motioning for Davis and me to follow, Holmes led us back into the corridor through which we had just passed. Across the hallway, a door stood half open, affording a partial view of a line of glass-fronted bookshelves. Like a row of mirrors, they reflected a series of dancing lights all originating from the clear chimney of a solitary hurricane lamp, which was positioned out of our sight somewhere on the other side of the room.

With fingers outstretched, Holmes pushed wide the door, and Davis and I followed him into what was obviously a library. Along the wall to our right stood a large mahogany desk, and upon it presided the single lamp whose reflection we had just noted.

It was not the lamp that demanded our attention, however; it was the scene illuminated by its glow: a young man in a turning-chair sat slumped forward across the burnished desktop, his head twisted in our direction. Immediately beneath his neck, a wide pool of blood had puddled on the dark-green blotter.

No medical expert was needed to point out that the victim's throat had been cut and that he was clearly dead. Though his eyes were closed and his skin appeared darkened by exposure to the weather, his straight nose, high cheekbones, and square jaw revealed a handsome face.

Carefully, Holmes made his way round the far side of the desk, drew from a pocket his magnifying lens, and turned up the lamp. Leaning over the scene, he worked from the outside in, examining the desktop first, then the body, and finally the wound.

"Who is he?" Davis demanded.

Holmes put a finger to his lips as he stood up. "Lower your voice. The murderer may still be about. We have to search further."

Yet entering the dining room served only to compound the horror. Stretched out on the floor by the side of a long oak table was the body of a young woman. She lay on her back, head turned towards the doorway. Between the strands of raven hair splayed across her placid face, translucent grey eyes stared off into nothingness.

She was dressed in a bright-orange kimono, its shortened sleeves exposing the whiteness of her bare arms. Open at the throat, the garment left exposed the sparkles of an intricate diamond necklace attached to a golden chain that encircled her neck. In comparison to her simple garb, the exquisite jewellery appeared out of place.

"Why," exclaimed Davis, "it's Miss Tamarova — the Russian woman from the train! And at her neck — that's — that's the necklace she stole from me!"

Holmes quieted him once more whilst I, upon ascertaining that she had no pulse, closed her eyes and moved away. It was then that Holmes began for a second time that night to scrutinise a deathly tableau.

First, he observed the immediate surroundings. The table near where she had fallen was laid for one; but close by on the white linen cloth were positioned a pair of cut-crystal wine glasses and a blue Wedgewood ashtray containing the butt-end of a single cigarette.

"Russian," observed Holmes after sniffing the tobacco. "*Makhorka* — a cheap, noxious blend." Dropping to his knees, he employed his lens to examine some additional flakes of cold cigarette ash on the floor.

(I too recognised the foul-smelling stuff. To my annoyance, it was the tobacco favoured by Holmes' friend, the elderly Russian detective, Porfiry Petrovitch.[1])

Next Holmes turned to the body itself. Even from where I was standing a few feet away, I could see at the swell of the woman's bosom the small knife-wound that vied for attention with the cluster of twinkling diamonds. Quite unlike the long, bloody cut that had taken the life of the young man, this simple incision just above the heart had left a thread-line of scarlet that disappeared down her side within the folds of the orange kimono.

---

[1] I first met Porfiry Petrovitch some ten years earlier in the case I titled *Sherlock Holmes and the Shadows of St. Petersburg*. Our investigation revisited the major success of the Russian detective's career, his solution to the murders described in Fyodor Dostoyevsky's *Crime and Punishment*. (JHW)

"You're certain it's the same necklace she took from you, Davis?" Holmes asked.

The American nodded.

My friend then proceeded to set his jaw, lean forward, and — to my great astonishment — snatch the diamonds from the dead woman's throat.

"Holmes!" I cried. "That's evidence you're disturbing."

"Whatever's gone on here," he said as he stuffed the necklace into his pocket, "at least we can return this bauble to its Royal owner. Besides, robbery was never the motive, or a diamond necklace like this one would not still be present."

"Thank you, Mr. Holmes," said an obviously relieved Richard Harding Davis. "That's a weight off my mind."

With the necklace now secure, we continued to search the rest of the house. Upon finding nothing else amiss, however, we felt confident in retracing our steps to the central hallway.

"Why not try the butler again?" Davis suggested.

It seemed like a reasonable plan; yet as soon as we returned to the sitting room, we discovered we had left open the outer door and that during the interim the butler had fled.

"We have done all that we can," Holmes said. "Now it is time for the police," Producing his Acme police whistle from a coat pocket, he stepped out onto the small, fog-bound landing at the front of the house and brought the silver instrument to his lips. A long, high-pitched overtone split the night.

"Return with Watson to Baker Street," Holmes told the American. "From there you should be able to hire a cab for your hotel. We shall talk tomorrow."

In agreement, Davis and I set out. Though still a formidable challenge, making our way back through the fog to a more familiar setting was a trifle easier than groping in the blind during our walk to Boston Street. When we reached our destination, I helped Davis collect the travelling bag he had left in our rooms and then, in spite of all the murk in the air, managed to hail him a cab.

"The Bath Hotel!" I heard him shout to the driver.

Only after watching the lights of the hansom fade into the mist did I climb the stairs back up to our lodgings. It was well past midnight by the time I reached the sitting room, settled into an armchair, and awaited the return of Sherlock Holmes.

Chapter Two

The Gibson Man

What I admire most in men –
To sit opposite a mirror at dinner
and not look in it.
— Richard Harding Davis
Quoted in
The United Service

For a day that culminated in the discovery of two brutal murders, it had begun in a most commonplace manner. To illustrate the point, I present my reconstruction of the events which ultimately led us to the ill-fated house in Boston Street that gloomy December night in 1897.

i

During the final months of the year, the weather had presented a recurring *mélange* of thunderstorms, frost and fog. It came as no surprise, therefore, when in the early-morning hours of the day in question —Saturday, the 18th December — the Medusa-like tendrils of a cold, thick fog began feeling their way through the streets of the city. Destined to become a true "London Particular" — as only the most intense of London fogs were called by the city's proud but beleaguered inhabitants — this seemingly innocent mist marked the start of the dismal vapour that would cause us so much consternation later that night.

In order to avoid contact with the oily muck, Holmes and I supplied ourselves with an assortment of newspapers. We could always rely on prints like *The Times*, the *Telegraph*, and the *Morning Post* to command our attention for any number of hours — especially in front of a crackling fire on a cold winter's day.

Yet even as we were so occupied, the fog continued to build; and eventually we could see nothing beyond our windowpanes but the yellow muck swirling in the air and condensing into a greasy mixture upon the outer glass.

It was late in the afternoon when Billy, the page-boy, knocked at our door. Aware that I had played rugby for Blackheath in my younger years, the lad made a point of including among his professional responsibilities the task of keeping me apprised of the club's fortunes.

"Blackheath versus *Cardiff* . . . ," he announced, raising his high-pitched voice on the final two syllables as if he were articulating a question.

Ever hopeful for news of a Blackheath victory, I looked up in anticipation from the *Post's* social column.

"Cancelled," Billy intoned, addressing the interrogative that had never been asked. By way of explanation, he volunteered the word "fog"; but he need not have bothered. A look out our window was sufficient to reveal how impenetrable the stuff had become and, as a result, how foolish was my expectation that a match could even be played, let alone won. The ill-fated destiny of any rugby contest held in London that day should have been obvious.

Holmes, of course, paid no attention to Billy's announcement. The fortunes of Blackheath FC did not concern him — nor, for that matter, did those of any other rugby or football club. When the boy had concluded his report to me, Holmes peered at him over the page of *The Times* he had been reading. "Anything else?" he asked brusquely.

"Sorry, Mr. Holmes," Billy said with an embarrassed grin. "The news of the cancelled rugby made me forget the main reason I come up in the first place. There's a bloke — "

Holmes cocked an eyebrow.

" — a client, I should say, here to see you."

Holmes nodded, and with all due diligence Billy prepared to announce the visitor's name. The boy stood at attention by the open door and, tugging at the skirts of his short jacket, cleared his throat.

Before he could utter a single syllable, however, the client in question — he had been hovering impatiently in the hallway during the rugby discussion — thrust forward an ebony walking stick and, shunting young Billy to the side, strode presumptuously into our presence. So expertly had he secured the centre-stage of our sitting room that Holmes and I had scarcely time to rise.

As soon as he removed his short hat, of course, I recognised him immediately; for his was a face I had seen many times before. So striking were his features —the clean-shaven lantern-jaw, the middle-parted black hair, the broad shoulders — that they had been artfully idealised on the pages of a number of American periodicals and sometimes even the occasional front cover.

Usually posed opposite one of those beautiful "Gibson Girls" with their perfectly straight noses and wonderfully swept-up hair, our visitor appeared to be in his early thirties and the epitome of sartorial faddishness. In keeping with his reputation, he wore a dark, fur-lined frock coat between whose lapels one could discern the martial cut of heavy, brown tweeds and the ornamental, military-style, red silk-ribbons pinned above his left-breast pocket. No less than the black-leather band of a wristwatch poked out from beneath his left coat-sleeve.

"I believe," declaimed the fellow in the shrill, flat vowels of American English, "that I have the honour of addressing Mr. Sherlock Holmes and Dr. John Watson. Allow me to introduce myself. I am R —"

"Richard Harding Davis!" I cried out, only to discover that much to my embarrassment I had blurted his three names at the very same moment he had. "You are the American writer," I proclaimed, "the author of the new war novel, *Soldiers of Fortune.*" With a blush of self-consciousness at what may have sounded like what the Americans call "bootlicking", I added, "I have seen your likeness in the illustrations of Charles Dana Gibson."

Our visitor grinned approvingly. "Quite right, Doctor," said he, shaking first my hand, then Holmes', "though I must confess that Charlie Gibson is a good friend, and serving as his model was more in the line of a favour."

Whilst Davis and I conversed, young Billy remained near the door gazing steadfastly at the American. With a quick wave of the hand, Holmes had already dismissed the boy; yet the lad, well-accustomed to my friend's peremptory manner, lingered a moment longer to stare at the client who just moments before had so unceremoniously eased him aside. After all, one did not get the opportunity to observe the so-called "Gibson Man" in the flesh every day.

It required a second wave from Holmes to send Billy slowly inching backward into the corridor. The lad took one final look at the celebrated figure and then, carefully closing the door behind him, exited our rooms.

In fairness, Billy's gawping reaction to the handsome Richard Harding Davis mirrored that of the public at large. And yet one would be remiss to allow the American's dramatic appearance to overshadow his talents as a writer.

By the time Davis arrived at our door, he had already established himself as a successful journalist. And though his news reports in Philadelphia and New York papers along with his travel pieces from Central America, the American West, and the Mediterranean fortified his journalistic reputation, one cannot overlook the fact that within the world of *belles-lettres* the man was equally well known.

Owing to the heart-warming short stories he had penned — some featuring the impish office boy called Gallegher and others, the urbane New Yorker called Van Bibber — Davis had earned the appellation of "the American Kipling". His patriotic defence of the United States helped justify the comparison.

But as his correspondence from foreign locales indicated, Davis did not limit his focus to American subjects. He kept himself busy writing about the various places he visited. Take England, for instance. Like Kipling, he praised the pageantry of the British Empire. Just the previous June, I had read his enthusiastic descriptions of the Queen's Jubilee that had appeared in *Harper's*, an American magazine.

"You captured those heady days so well," I told him.

"Ah, yes," Davis nodded, "the Diamond Jubilee. Quite a celebration!"

Indeed, no Englishman could forget those exciting times. It was estimated that more than a million-and-a-half well-wishers had invaded the city to mark Queen Victoria's sixty years of rule. Multi-coloured banners; tiered, wooden scaffolding; and red-coated soldiers had lined the Queen's six-mile parade route through the heart of the city. Why, some buildings had actually been razed to accommodate the teeming hordes of cheering spectators. It seemed that all of London — all of England, really — had gone mad. And Davis had captured it all.

"You do know," he said, his voice rising with renewed energy, "that even though I was reporting the proceedings for the American press, I was also asked to do so by your *London Times*." He nodded at Holmes' discarded newspaper lying upon an end table.

I raised my eyebrows in appreciation whilst Holmes merely sighed. I knew my friend well enough to sense that he had exceeded his fill of prattle for the afternoon.

But Richard Harding Davis was not yet done. "Oh, yes," he went on, "*The Times* had been impressed by my war-reporting in Greece, you see. But, alas, I had already committed to *Harper's* for the Jubilee, and I'm sure you gentlemen will agree that keeping your word is always the right thing to do. As my mother[2] would say, one really has no other choice."

Sherlock Holmes would concur with such a philosophy, of course; but at that moment he was more inclined to discover the nature of his new client's business.

"I am afraid, Mr. Davis," said Holmes, "that what entertains friend Watson often leaves me cold. I assume that you have come here on some matter of urgency, and I suggest that you reveal it poste-haste."

We had been conducting our conversation whilst standing awkwardly at the centre of the room; and Holmes, upon completing his last sentence, ushered Davis towards an armchair in front of the fire.

The American proceeded in that direction; but before taking his seat, he removed from where it was slung across his shoulder a brown, leather satchel, which — given the drama of his entrance — I had scarcely noticed. He handed it, along with his frock coat, short hat, and ebony walking stick, to me. Only then did he settle into the designated chair.

---

[2] Davis' mother, author Rebecca Harding Davis (1831-1910), was known for her muckraking fiction about political corruption, racial injustice, and the travails of the working class. She inculcated Richard with a strong sense of fair play. (DDV)

"In spite of the fog," he announced whilst I was hanging his hat and coat on the pegs near the door, "I have come directly from King's Cross. You see, gentlemen, I'm well aware of your reputation for solving problems; and I can think of no more appropriate chaps to settle things for me. I'm here to tell you, I face matters that demand immediate attention, matters most disturbing."

"'Disturbing'?" I repeated as I placed his stick and bag against the wall beneath his coat.

At first glance, the man appeared in such fine fettle that it was difficult to envision him disturbed by anything. And yet once I had seated myself opposite him, I could detect the tiny lines of worry at the corners of his keen eyes and at the edges of his dry lips. It was then also that I observed a tremor in his right leg.

Davis noted the direction of my gaze and began rubbing his palm along his thigh. "Sciatica," he explained. "It afflicts me at the oddest moments. It's one reason for the stick I carry. You never know when it will come in handy."

If Davis' grand entrance had hampered my own assessment of his constitution, it seemed a certainty that Sherlock Holmes had penetrated the histrionic posing as soon as the man had stepped inside the door. Yet whatever theories my perceptive friend might have already concocted, I believe that not even he was prepared for Davis' next few words: "The unfortunate story I am about to relate, Mr. Holmes, actually begins with your brother Mycroft."

"My brother, you say!" With as much filial curiosity as professional interest, Holmes focused his steel-grey eyes more intently on the American.

"Right," said Davis, eagerly welcoming the renewed attention, "your brother, Mr. Mycroft Holmes. Although his participation was relatively minor, it actually marked the beginning of my trouble."

Holmes' expression remained stoic, but he leaned forward in his chair. For my part, I was appreciating just how much Richard Harding Davis liked to talk. Discounting his roundabout approach to beginning a narrative, I sensed he had an intriguing story to tell.

"I left England for the States at the end of this past summer," Davis recounted. "By that time I had already reported on the Tsar's coronation in Moscow, the Millennial Celebration in Budapest, and your Queen's Jubilee here in London. When I finally got back to New York, I decided that after working as a reporter for so long, I would change direction and rekindle my interest in theatre. In a nutshell, gentlemen, I planned to write a play based on my latest novel."

"*Soldiers of Fortune*," I offered.

"You've read it?"

"Alas, not yet," I confessed, though I was aware that the book dealt with the quashing of a workers' rebellion against American business interests in a Central American country.

"In truth," said Davis. "I was hoping for the same kind of success that Will Gillette had with *Secret Service* a couple of years ago.[3] You'll recall that the Prince of Wales went to see Gillette's production at the Adelphi last spring when it was performed here in London."

In fairness, I did not recall the Prince's attendance at such a performance, though I seemed to have retained some dim memory of a melodrama related to the American Civil War. Quite frankly, a theatrical work about so provincial a topic held little interest for me.

It seemed to hold little interest for Sherlock Holmes as well. He slumped back in his chair and closed his eyes — though whether he was bored or concentrating all the more was difficult to tell.

As for Davis, he did not seem to notice. He went on about his theatre plans. "A deal like Gillette's is the kind of thing I'm shooting for. And to be honest, back in New York I wasn't receiving much encouragement. For whatever the reason, I felt incapable of achieving my goal there. I guess I lacked the proper motivation."

"A pity," I said.

---

[3] Though we could not know it at the time, the celebrated American actor and playwright William Gillette would continue his success two years later by portraying the eponymous lead in the play he had written titled *Sherlock Holmes*. (JHW)

"Not to worry, Doctor. For it was then that I remembered how thoroughly I had enjoyed my summer in this glorious city. And that's not even to mention the trips I made here in '89 and '92. London has always symbolised adventure and romance to me, so I figured that coming back would be just the tonic to stimulate my creative juices."

I could certainly understand Davis' state of mind. The curious byways and mysterious inhabitants of London have never failed to furnish me with inspiration.

"I wound up returning to England a couple of weeks ago," Davis continued, "on the first of December, to be exact. And it was only a few days after my arrival here in London that I received a message from Robert Stanton."

At a relevant new fact, Holmes opened his eyes. "And who is this Robert Stanton?" he asked.

"A good question, Mr. Holmes, since the man has so many connections. Lieutenant Robert Stanton is the *aide-de-camp* for the American naval attaché to the court of Russia. I met him in May of last year in Moscow at the coronation of the Tsar. We discovered each other in a line of *étrangers de distinction* — you know, important people — awaiting early admission to the festivities inside the Kremlin.

"Oh, dear," I could imagine Holmes thinking, "another long-winded story."

"Stanton was part of the American legation," Davis went on, "and — at least, as far as I could tell —the only one I'd met who'd actually read *Soldiers of Fortune.* One thing led to another, and soon enough we discovered that we both belonged to the same club in Westminster.

"'You know,' I told him, hoping for the sympathy of a fellow member, 'to a clubless American, London can be a most inhospitable city.'

"'You're right about that,' he said sympathetically.

"That was when I informed him that I lacked a ticket to the Tsar's coronation. The ceremony was to be held inside the Church of the Assumption. They call it a cathedral, but it actually looks more like a chapel, and seating was at quite a premium. I had already tried all my tricks with the authorities — even bribery — but to no avail.

"I don't know how Stanton did it, but one way or another, my fellow clubber used his influence with Clifton Breckinridge, our Minister to Russia, to get me one of those little blue admission badges. There must have been a hundred members of the press who weren't so fortunate."[4]

"A bit too Machiavellian for my taste," I said.

With impatience undercutting his tone, Holmes sat up straight and asked once more, "But what does this Lieutenant Stanton have to do with the matter at hand?"

"Background," Davis said. "I want you to understand that even though his military responsibilities require him to work in Russia, Stanton knows important people. As luck would have it, he happened to return to London at about the same time I did. Hearing through the Embassy of my arrival,

---

[4] For Davis' written account of the coronation, see his *A Year From a Reporter's Notebook.* (DDV)

he contacted me at the Bath Hotel to renew our comradeship."

"All very interesting, I'm sure, Mr. Davis," said Sherlock Holmes, "but how does any of it relate to my brother? You said your story began with him."

Davis raised his hands, palms outward, in self-defence. "Hold your horses, Mr. Holmes," he said. "I'm getting there. It turned out that when the highest levels of your government learned that Stanton and I knew each other, he was asked to inform me that one Mycroft Holmes — 'the brother of the famous detective,' was how Stanton put it — had requested a meeting with me at the High Table. That's the club in Westminster where Stanton and I are both members."

"The High Table?" I repeated. "Never heard of it." And yet if this Lieutenant Stanton conducted meetings involving Mycroft Holmes in such a place, one could only guess what other important activities went on there as well.

Sherlock Holmes provided me no opportunity for further questions. "Mr. Davis," said he in exasperation, "perhaps we might at last get to the nub. Why did Mycroft wish to see you?"

Davis smiled again. "Quite simple, really. Your brother had a sensitive task that wanted completing, and he asked for my help. It seems that the Queen wanted —"

"The Queen, you say?" Holmes interrupted. "Her participation adds an additional layer of concern. Was there anyone else in the club besides you, my brother, and Stanton who might have overheard your conversation?"

"Funny you should ask, Mr. Holmes," Davis replied. "There was this fellow in the smoking room, a middle-aged man with an elaborate moustache— another club member I presumed. I remember that he wore a single black-pearl stud in his shirt; it was quite a handsome piece. Anyway, this fellow, once the three of us had seated ourselves in an alcove off to the side, had the nerve to position himself in the corridor just beyond our view."

"It was your brother who noticed him. 'Do you intend to come in, Sir Roderick?' your brother asked. But the man leaned forward, waved a farewell, and retreated to the smoking room. At least, as far as I could tell that's where he went. That was the last I saw of him."

Holmes nodded. "And the nature of Mycroft's business? Her Majesty, you said —"

"Yes, The Queen. The Queen desired to send a diamond necklace to a friend. Apparently, it was to be an early Christmas present."

Holmes and I could attest to Her Majesty's affinity for bestowing jewellery as gifts. At Windsor Castle two years before, she had awarded Sherlock Holmes an emerald tiepin for his work in retrieving the stolen plans for the Bruce-Partington submarine.

"Who was to be the fortunate recipient of the Queen's largess?" Holmes wanted to know.

"Lady Brownlow, wife to the Earl of Brownlow. They live in Belton House, near Grantham."

"In Lincolnshire," Holmes added.

"Right you are, Mr. Holmes. Thanks to my friendship with Harry Cust, the Earl's nephew, I've actually spent some time with the family there. I palled around with old Harry in Oxford a few years ago. I even travelled along on his campaign for Parliament — which he won, by the way."

"The diamond necklace?" Holmes prompted.

Davis nodded. "When the Queen was informed that I frequently undertook the railroad journey north, she thought that I would be the perfect person to convey such a piece of jewellery without raising attention. I humbly add that she praised my reputation for rectitude."

Holmes and I exchanged sceptical glances at what both of us already suspected to be misguided commendation.

"Surely," I protested, "one of the Queen's messengers could have filled the role. Or maybe — if an American was desired — even your friend, Stanton. Someone with military training, I should expect."

"Apparently not, Doctor. At least, your brother didn't think so. He seemed quite insistent on the subject of anonymity — not that I am anonymous, of course" — here he offered a self-serving bow of the head — "but to be fair, transporting valuables is not my usual line of work."

Sherlock Holmes leaned forward again. "And just how, Mr. Davis, did this bauble come to be stolen from you?"

Davis' eyes opened wide. "But — but how did you guess it was stolen?"

Holmes shook his head at the man's obtuseness.

"Perhaps your brother —?"

"Mycroft has told me nothing; admitting errors does not come easily to the Holmes family. Nor does guessing.

Actually, Mr. Davis, my reasoning is elementary. You spoke of a disturbing matter. You have already told us that in spite of the fog, you came here today immediately upon arriving at King's Cross. Your leather handbag proves the point. And yet you have been here for close to half an hour and have not got round to discussing what has prompted your visit."

"But I —" Davis attempted to interrupt, yet Holmes went right on.

"Though it was you who brought up the story of the necklace, Mr. Davis, you have so far managed to talk about everything but — the Queen's Jubilee, the Tsar's Coronation, even parliamentary elections. One can only presume that something untoward has happened to the necklace — a detail which makes the circumstance difficult to explain. My experience in such matters suggests that it has disappeared."

"Well, yes, but —" Davis tried again.

"Please, Mr. Davis, it is quite obvious that as reluctant to face the facts as you appear to be, you feel responsible for the loss. Logic suggests the event which you have so far avoided describing is the theft of the very diamond necklace entrusted to you for safekeeping by Her Majesty."

Davis looked uncomfortable. He took a deep breath and through pursed lips blew out the air that had filled his reddening cheeks. Then he leaned forward and ran his hands through his straight, black hair.

"You're quite right about the theft, Mr. Holmes," he said at last. "You are also correct to identify me as the responsible party — the one who allowed this unhappy circumstance to occur — and consequently the person upon whom it is incumbent to set matters right."

"Finally," observed Holmes, "we are making progress."

Davis sat up straight and faced us both. "That's why I've come to see you, gentlemen," said he. "With your help, I hope to recover the stolen item as quickly as possible. It's the only honourable solution." The man seemed as rigid in his righteousness as he was in his posture.

Sherlock Holmes steepled his fingers beneath his chin and leaned back in his armchair. "How were you conveying the necklace?"

Davis smiled. "Perhaps you know of the French writer, Victorien Sardou. I'm fascinated by the theatre, you see; and it was his play, *Les Pattes de Mouche* — that suggested to me the idea of hiding something in plain sight."

"Yes, yes, I know the play," Holmes said impatiently. "In English, *A Scrap of Paper*. Clever though it may be, the concept is an appropriation. The deception caused by 'hiding something in plain sight'—as you put it—was popularised earlier by your own countryman, Edgar Allan Poe."

"Gentlemen," I felt compelled to interject, "we are getting far afield. Mr. Davis, I believe you were preparing to tell us how you transported the necklace."

"Quite so," Holmes muttered, glancing at me and then at Davis, who sat up even straighter.

"Let me try again," said the American. "You are quite correct, Mr. Holmes, to accuse me of avoiding my responsibilities."

Holmes nodded. Confirming his opinion never failed to appease him.

Davis cleared his throat as he began once more. "I am a smoker, gentlemen, one who enjoys a good cigar as well as the next man, and I was looking forward to a quiet smoke in the train to Lincolnshire. With faith in Sardou's — or Poe's — belief in concealing something in the open, I sought a method for doing just that.

"As a result, I purchased two identical cigar cases. Here is one." He drew from inside his coat pocket a wallet-sized case of brown leather containing a handful of small cheroots. White stitching framed its edges.

Holmes put out his palm, and Davis handed the case to him.

"One of these cases," Davis explained whilst Holmes proceeded to turn the container this way and that, "was to be the noticeable hiding place, and it was into that one that I slipped the necklace. That was the case I left in my inner coat pocket — relatively speaking, in plain sight. After all, who could possibly imagine that a cigar case containing anything valuable would be left so accessible?"

"Who indeed?" said Sherlock Holmes, cocking an eyebrow whilst disdainfully tossing the case back to its owner.

"An admirable act of subterfuge," I offered in sympathetic defence.

"It seems that Fate was less appreciative than you, Doctor," said Davis. "You see, knowing I would want to smoke during the train ride to Lincolnshire, I placed my actual cigars in the other case, the one I kept out of sight. Since it wouldn't do to have two cigar cases out in the open, I stowed the case with the cigars next to my writing materials — paper, pens, and the like — at the bottom of the satchel." He nodded in the direction of the leather bag he had entrusted to me earlier. "Out of sight, but easily reachable."

Now I was beginning to understand. One did not have to be Sherlock Holmes to envision the unravelling of Davis' so-called plan — what would obviously turn out to be his not-so-clever attempt at subterfuge.

"When did you leave for Lincolnshire?" Holmes asked.

"Why, early this morning. From King's Cross. And before you ask, I told no one of my schedule, not even Stanton or your brother."

"Did you travel alone?" I wanted to know.

"That was my intention, Doctor," said Davis, his leg beginning to shake again. "In fact, I had paid for a private compartment. But just moments after the train had lurched forward to begin its run, the carriage door burst open, a blast of cold air blew over me, and a small Gladstone bag came flying in from the outside. It landed at my feet. At the same time, the train was picking up speed; and as the door continued to hang open, I could see a young woman, presumably the owner of the Gladstone, running desperately alongside.

"She was reaching out to grasp the door handle, which as she ran, was receding before her fingertips. The drop-off at the end of the platform was rapidly approaching, and there were only seconds to spare."

"My word," I gasped. "What happened next?"

"Without any thought, I sprang up, gripped the metal doorframe with my left hand, and leaned out as far as I could, straining with my right to grab the woman's outstretched arm. The icy wind whipped at my face; but just as the carriage was about to streak past the end of the platform, our hands connected, and I pulled her to safety inside the compartment."

"Good show!" I cried with a burst of applause.

"A young woman, you say?" Holmes asked determinedly. "What was her appearance?"

Davis' face lit up. "Why, quite handsome, actually. She wore a long black coat, her dark hair was wrapped in a white shawl; and though her face was flushed, she had the most beautiful blue-grey eyes."

Holmes grunted — as if it was exactly the kind of response he had anticipated.

In light of Davis' heroic rescue, I confess that it was the same answer I too was anticipating.

iii

Holmes' and my expectations to the contrary, Richard Harding Davis focused less on the woman's appearance than on her condition.

"In point of fact," he recounted, "the poor creature was so out of breath that she had to sit for a few minutes gulping air. As her shoulders rose and fell, it was cold enough in the compartment to see each exhalation. She must have run some distance before catching up to the train."

"As that may be, Mr. Davis," Holmes countered, "you were conveying precious cargo, the Queen's necklace. Why did you not appeal to a porter to have her moved to another compartment or carriage?"

Davis tried to pull a serious face, but almost immediately a close-lipped grin undermined his effort. "As my mother taught me, gentlemen, always try to do right when it comes to dealing with women. And just as I write to her every day, I couldn't see ignoring her advice. No, I knew I would make every effort to aid that desperate creature as soon as I saw her running alongside the train. How could I not help her come aboard?"

"One dares to say," I ventured, "that the fact she was attractive also argued in her favour."

"The fairer sex need never apologise for their appearance," countered the American, "as long as it is in keeping with decorum. I do confess that she had a beautiful face and the most luxuriant raven tresses. What's more, though she was wrapped in a long wool coat, I could sense that she was trim of stature as well."

"Trim of stature indeed," Holmes muttered. "But her charms aside, Mr. Davis, did it not occur to you that this woman might somehow have got wind of the necklace you were carrying? You yourself suggested you might have been overheard at your club by the fellow with the moustache. She could have followed you to King's Cross and made her dramatic last-minute entrance in such a fashion as to allow you no opportunity to cast her out."

Davis batted Holmes' charge away with the flick of his wrist. "Tosh, man, she didn't even know who I was. At least, I don't think she did. She spoke with a Russian accent. And, if you can believe it, she actually mistook me for your English actor, George Alexander. Fancy that!"

I narrowed my eyes in search of the resemblance. Alexander may have been a shade older than Davis, but both were handsome young men with similarly parted hair and strong, masculine chins. Because the actor's face frequently appeared in the public prints, there was every reason to believe that the young woman could have seen his picture and confused him with the American writer.

"Imagine not recognising this profile," said Davis as he turned his head to the side to show off his straight nose and square jaw. "On the contrary, gentlemen, I offer no excuses for helping her. I made certain she was comfortable, and then I placed her bag on the small shelf above her seat opposite mine."

Holmes sighed in exasperation. "Pray continue your narrative, Mr. Davis —though one can readily see where it is heading."

"Indeed," Davis murmured sadly. "Yes. Well, as I said, I had hoped to smoke on the train. Before the arrival of the woman, I figured that I could easily get to the cigars I had stored in my handbag. But with this new passenger now in the compartment, I couldn't risk any moves involving my cigar cases."

"Quite right," said I. "But at least you could appreciate that you were sparing the young lady the discomfort of unwanted fumes from your cheroot."

"Discomfort," Davis repeated drily. "On the contrary, Doctor. It was she who brought up the very issue. After we had exhausted any number of pleasantries regarding the rigours of travel, the chill in the air, and the nature of our destinations, she actually asked me, 'Do you mind if I smoke?'

"With alacrity in my heart and sympathy in my smile, I immediately nodded my approval.

"In response, she produced a black reticule from her coat pocket and drew out a small packet of cigarettes. As it turned out, they contained a pungent Russian tobacco. *'Makhorka'* she called it and held the packet out to me. 'Be careful,' she cautioned. 'The tobacco is very strong, a preference I gained from my father.'"

"We are familiar with the blend," Holmes noted with a scowl, no doubt recalling the malodorous tobacco favoured by his friend, the Russian detective.

Davis allowed himself a laugh. "Then you can well imagine, Mr. Holmes, the stink we created in that tiny railway compartment! With no cigar as an alternative, I eagerly accepted her offer and struck a single match for the two of us. For the next quarter hour we indulged ourselves, sedately puffing away."

I could picture the pair, Davis and the alluring Russian woman, confined in a railway carriage full of thick, rank smoke as the train, swaying back and forth, huffed its way up the incline beyond King's Cross.

And later, with London and its icy slate roofs behind them and the clouds of tobacco haze cleared, I could imagine the young woman gazing out the window at the frigid countryside — smoke rising from the chimneys of the few houses near the railway, naked trees raising leafless limbs laced in frost, Holsteins huddling together for warmth — and the young American seated opposite engaged in watching her do so.

"She told me that her name was Miss Tamarova," Davis said, "that she lived in London, and that she was travelling to Nottingham to see her sister. At Grantham, my own destination on the way to Belton House, she intended to board the Nottingham train.

"By the time we reached the flatlands of Peterborough — about half the distance to Grantham — all still seemed in order. When it was announced that the train would linger there for a few minutes, Miss Tamarova announced she would go inside the station to send her sister a telegram. 'I shall tell her of my progress,' she said, arranging the white shawl to cover a few uncooperative strands of hair.

"Once she was gone, I reasoned that I could finally get to my cigars. In order to move about more freely, I took the opportunity provided by the woman's absence to remove my coat. Next, I proceeded to retrieve my cigars in the leather case that I'd hidden away in the satchel. When I laid my coat on the seat, however, the other case — the one containing the necklace — slipped out of my pocket and fell onto the cushion. 'Not to worry,' I said to myself as I bent over to pick it up.

"At that very moment, however, the door to the carriage opened, and I was barely able to restore the cases to their rightful places. As if it matters, in spite of my breakneck manoeuvring, I was able to retain a cigar for a final smoke during the last leg of our trip."

The convivial smile now left Davis' lips. "I suppose I didn't correctly position my satchel on the cushion. I did manage to put my coat on and regain my seat; but when the train started up, the lurch of the carriage not only caused Miss Tamarova to drop her reticule and its contents to spill out at her feet, but also served to tumble my bag to the floor. As I rose to help her collect her belongings — well, she turned her attention to retrieving mine. It was then that we actually collided.

"'Sorry,' we both said at the same time and with a mutual giggle exchanged our properties. In the moments that followed, I slipped my hand inside my coat as surreptitiously as possible to verify that I still retained my valuable cigar case — that it had not been pickpocketed by this strange woman during our collision. Once I felt its comforting leather ridges, I lit my cigar and leaned back to enjoy the rest of the journey."

Holmes shook his head.

"Soon the train began the gentle climb up the lime ridge approaching Grantham, and I knew it was just a matter of minutes before we reached the railroad yard. As the train began to slow, Miss Tamarova sought to collect her Gladstone. 'Would you be so kind,' she said, nodding in the direction of the shelf above her head. I rose to reach her bag, but — as if there had been some miscommunication — she rose at the same time, and we collided again.

"I apologised once more, but no sooner did I hand her the Gladstone than to my utter and complete astonishment she flung wide the compartment door — mind you, the train was still moving — and leaped out onto the platform in front of the red-brick station. An instant later and she had disappeared somewhere beyond the building. It was as if she were playing out in reverse her dramatic entrance into the compartment at the start of the trip.

"I stood in wonder for a minute or two until it finally dawned on me that she was in the process of making some sort of escape. I panicked then, I tell you, but only for a moment. One touch of my pocket assured me that the cigar case with the diamond necklace still remained.

"Not until I looked into my bag did I discover that that she-devil had somehow managed to pilfer the other case, the one with the cigars hidden inside it. But true tragedy had been averted; my ruse had worked. I may have been robbed of some good smokes, but I still possessed the cigar case containing the valuable necklace. That case, the one within easy reach inside my coat, had gone untouched. At least, it's what I believed just then. In contrast to what might have happened, I felt relieved. Nothing to get upset about."

"You were lucky," I said whilst Sherlock Holmes allowed himself a quick smile.

"Yeah," Davis muttered, "lucky — or so I thought at the time. But just to be on the safe side, I decided to check that I still had the necklace. As I've said, the case was there all right, with its leather ridges and white stitching; but when I opened it up — well, Mr. Holmes, you know what I found."

"Cigars," Holmes proclaimed.

"Yes. Quite right. It was the case I just showed you. I believe I must have accidentally switched the cases when I was returning them to their hiding places. That woman chose the right case by mistake."

"The one in plain sight," I could not prevent myself from saying.

"Which," Holmes pointed out, "the beguiling Russian woman might have known about by secretly watching you through the carriage window at the station when she was supposed to be off telegraphing her sister."

Davis nodded. "Indeed — though however it happened, it is up to me to retrieve the necklace — without involving the authorities." Now he turned to face Holmes directly. "I have to get it back, Mr. Holmes. It's the only way I can avoid giving your brother bad news. As I've already said, it's the reason I've come here — for your help in recovering the stolen necklace."

"Understood," my friend answered. "For my part, I would like to spare my brother the distasteful job of having to report to a certain august lady that her diamond necklace has been lost. So what more can you tell us of this Miss Tamarova?"

Davis furrowed his brow as if plumbing the depths of his memory. Suddenly, he cried out, "I just remembered — Baker Street's near Regent's Park, isn't it?"

"A few minutes' walk," I replied

"Well, you know, she said something about enjoying her walks to Regent's Park. She mentioned a house — No. 11, if I remember correctly — on Boston Road — or was it Boston Square? I can't recall. I remember the Boston part because of our city in Massachusetts."

"Boston *Street*, actually," I advised. "It's not far from here, just off the Park Road, which skirts the southwest edge of the park itself."

"That must be it!" cried Davis. "She said there was a black-rail fence with small, white columns in front."

"Foolish girl," Holmes muttered, "giving out such information. Obvious proof she is an amateur." Holmes rose and moved in the direction of the door. "Join us for a brief dinner, Mr. Davis," he offered. "Then we shall attempt to make our way through this infernal fog to Boston Street. Assuming Miss Tamarova told you the truth about living there, perhaps we can find her — or at least a neighbour who might point out her house."

Following those words, Holmes hurried into the corridor just beyond our sitting room. Leaning over the bannister railing, he shouted down the staircase.

"Mrs. Hudson! Sandwiches for three! Quickly, if you please!"

iv

Had we been more expeditious, we might have prevented the two murders — though, of course, we could not have known it at the time. Even so, we wolfed down the beefsteak sandwiches Billy had delivered from Mrs. Hudson. She had made them on short notice, but then our much-tested landlady was quite used to Holmes' eccentric demands.

By half seven, we were ready to pursue our quarry. Davis reclaimed his walking stick; and the three of us, after donning thick coats, woollen scarves, and our respective headwear — Holmes, his deerstalker; Davis, his short hat; and I, my bowler — stepped out to face the elements.

Immediately upon exiting the outer door, however, we came to an abrupt halt. Indeed, it was all we could do to avoid crashing into one another like a dominoes-line of circus clowns. A dense curtain of oily fog confronted us in the darkness, the same muck I described at the start of this narrative. One could see no farther than the proverbial hand in front of one's face — except that in this instance the hand was anything but proverbial.

"I'm impressed," observed Davis drolly. "A fog like this makes the ones in New York look like sunshine."

It certainly appeared formidable. "Perhaps we should wait for more favourable conditions," I suggested.

"No!" Davis fairly shouted. "You said yourself, Mr. Holmes that Boston Street is not too far. We need to solve this riddle as quickly as possible."

Holmes agreed, and I wrapped my scarf more securely round my neck. Then, accompanied by the tap of Davis' walking stick, the three of us set off Indian-file into the thick, dark mist.

With Holmes in the lead, we headed north along Baker Street in the direction of Park Road. Though the widely-spaced gas lamps served to mark our snail-like progress, we could discern their illuminating auras only after we had arrived within a few feet of them. Rendered invisible by the fog, their supportive posts made the yellow orbs seem to float eerily in mid-air.

We shuffled northward along the west side of the street, skimming the fingers of our left hands against the moist, black-metal railings that fronted the houses. Normally, one could cover the distance between our rooms and Boston Street in a matter of minutes; but tonight our need to maintain contact with the fencing would make the trek last considerably longer.

The terminus of Upper Baker Street presented new challenges. Not only did we have to take care not to bypass the turning into Park Road as we bore northwest, but with the Baker Street railing ending before the turning, we had to concentrate on staying together.

With great caution we inched forward. A wrong turn by any one of us could cast that unfortunate into a night's worth of solitary wandering—or worse, should he happen to stumble into the menacing roadway somewhere off to our right. To be sure, the odd carriage-light floating through the ether or the muted rumble of growlers driving ever so slowly down the road seemed harmless enough; but fall under the hooves of the horses pulling those carriages, and the results could be fatal.

The muffled staccato of Davis' walking stick helped Holmes and me keep the American between us. But constant talking, Holmes assured us, would confirm our proximity with even greater certainty.

"The perfect opportunity, Mr. Davis," said I, my voice strangely deadened by the fog, "for you to tell us more about The High Table. Why was it there, I wonder, that you met with Lieutenant Stanton and Mycroft Holmes?"

"I guess," said he, his voice, equally muffled, "that such a question implies you didn't know that Mycroft Holmes is also a member."

Mycroft a member of the High Table? Had I heard correctly? I knew of his membership in the Diogenes; but as the biographer of Mycroft's brother, I imagined that so significant a detail about the membership of my subject's closest relative in an influential club should have previously been made known to me by Holmes himself.

"It's true, Watson," Holmes offered from somewhere in front of us. He spoke loudly to be sure his voice carried, and his tone contained not a hint of remorse at having excluded this information from my knowledge of his family. "Mycroft joined the High Table a few years ago after he gained his pre-eminent position within the government.

Membership provided not only a feather in Mycroft's cap, but also significant political contacts. What is more, the place is particularly convenient for him since it is just down the road from his digs."

"That's right," said Davis. "The High Table allows only people of the greatest distinction to enter its ranks. I'm not much of a joiner myself; but when I was invited to be an honorary member, you bet I was quick to agree. I think it was the war reporting I'd done in Greece that opened the door."

At that moment a fellow pedestrian, this one in a flat cap and mac, emerged from the murk. During such foggy nights, one encountered other walkers only intermittently. Like ghosts, they would pop out of the mist and then just as quickly de-materialise as they passed us by.

"The High Table is set up to be quite sociable," Davis continued once the apparition had vanished. "In the central dining room there's only one long table, and anyone sitting at it is compelled by the rules to engage in conversation with anyone else, known or unknown, seated nearby."

"Strange," I said. "I do not recall social intercourse being one of Mycroft's strong suits."

"Quite so, Watson," Holmes called back. "Mycroft enjoys the perquisites the High Table offers, but not its regulations. Indeed, I should imagine that without the High Table, the Diogenes — which, as you may recall, Mycroft helped establish — would never have come into being. The members of the Diogenes, Mr. Davis, are not allowed to speak to one another."

"No need to worry," said Davis. "The rules of the High Table aren't set in stone. As I already told you, it was in an alcove off to the side where we conducted our business concerning the necklace."

Just then, we reached the end of the metal railings; and with a small road to cross, the three of us became silent. We were approaching our destination now; and untethered for a second time as we ventured off the kerb and into the roadway, we found our slow pace growing even slower.

It seemed an eternity until we touched metal fencing again and even longer before I felt the smooth narrow wall of a pilaster. I could only hope we had reached the railing and columns that Davis had reported as fronting the string of connected-houses in Boston Street.

And yet in so thick a fog as that which then enveloped us, one could never be completely certain of the proper path. We might assume we were passing row- houses on our left, and yet a wrong turn here or a mistaken swerve there could have placed us somewhere else entirely.

Why, we might have been standing on the verge of Regent's Park or within the Park itself or even — one shudders to contemplate — within its celebrated Zoological Gardens. A mere few steps beyond, a hungry lion might be licking his chops at the approach the three innocents stumbling through the masking fog.

It was at that moment, however, that the rectangular light from the open doorway at No. 11 caught our attention and, beacon-like, attracted us to the mysterious house of death with which this narrative began.

Chapter Three

The Day After

i

On the Saturday night that we encountered the two dead bodies in Boston Street, Sherlock Holmes did not return to our rooms until a few minutes past two o'clock. It had taken that long for him to complete his discussions with the police concerning our grim discoveries.

"So late?" I asked, greeting him with a pot of hot chocolate in hand.

"Indeed," said Holmes as he rid himself of his outer garb. "As soon as the constable who had heard my whistle finally arrived, I gave him a message for Scotland Yard. And even with an experienced driver, it took Lestrade another hour in the fog to reach the place."

"How did you explain our appearance at the scene of a double-murder?" I asked, pouring him a cup of the hot chocolate.

"I told Lestrade that we were accompanying the reporter, Richard Harding Davis, to Boston Street to meet a young woman whom Davis had encountered on a train. That it was in her house that we found the bodies. Lest you worry, old fellow, I spared the Inspector the details about the necklace."

"And did he accept your explanation?"

"Lestrade?" Holmes laughed drily. "Imagination has never been his strong suit, and he found it difficult to believe that someone might venture out in such a fog for nothing more than a social engagement. Still, after surveying the premises he let me go. We'll deal with the aftermath tomorrow once the weather has cleared."

In spite of the lateness of the hour, Holmes and I clinked our cups together and savoured the hot brew. Yet once they were empty, I for one was quite ready for sleep. Climbing the stairs to my bedroom, however, I could see that Holmes was still not prepared to retire. When I last caught sight of him, he was moving towards the small table upon which still lay the day's newspapers.

The air remained chill Sunday morning, but at least the fog had dissipated during the night. I concluded as much from the shards of sunlight piercing the windows of the sitting room. Holmes greeted me at the breakfast table in his mouse-coloured dressing gown. Spread out next to his plate lay a copy of Saturday's *Times*. It was opened to page three.

"Look here, Watson," said he, bringing his forefinger down on one article in particular. It was headed "Missing Heir Returns".

"This is the very story I was reading when Davis called on us yesterday. At the time, it appeared to contain little of relevance; today it speaks volumes."

With a buttered scone in hand, I stood next to Holmes and perused the initial paragraphs:

There was good news to report on the docks of Southampton early Friday morning. Stepping onto English soil after an absence of more than a year was the Earl of Ingraham — that is, Rochester Ingraham, the elder son of the Marquis of Putnam.

Contact with the Earl had been lost months ago after he had undertaken a mountain-climbing excursion in South America. Though an accomplished climber and member of the Alpine Club of Savile Row, Lord Ingraham was rumoured

to have fallen to his death from a rigorous peak near
Quito, Ecuador . . . .[5]

I paused to take a bite of the scone. "I'm happy the Earl of Ingraham has been discovered alive, Holmes," said I, settling into my seat across from my friend, "but what in the world has it to do with us?"

Holmes lifted the silver-plated coffee-pot, poured himself a cup, and added two cubes of sugar. "Last night," said he, "whilst awaiting the arrival of the police, I was able to inspect the pockets of the dead man. During my search, I discovered a note in which Cyril Ingraham, the younger brother of the recently returned Lord Ingraham, agreed to a meeting the two had planned for earlier that evening in Walsingham House."

"Walsingham House!" I cried out. "Why, that's in Piccadilly! Next door to the Bath Hotel where Davis is staying."

"Quite so," said Holmes, "though presumably an unrelated fact. The note, on the other hand, serves to identify the body in question; the dead man we discovered is the very

---

[5] It would be another few years before Holmes and I had personal dealings with the Alpine Club. That case, which I called "An Adventure in Darkness", put us in touch with a climber who had actually visited the so-called "Country of the Blind", the benighted community that H.G. Wells described to a world-wide reading audience in 1911. (JHW) Watson's account may be found in *Sherlock Holmes: Adventures in the Realms of H.G. Wells (Vol. 1)* edited by Derrick Belanger. (DDV)

person about whom you have just been reading — Rochester Ingraham, the elder son and heir to the Marquis of Putnam."

"Good God. Are you quite certain?"

"Oh, yes," said Holmes pausing to sip his coffee. "The deceased is the same personage presumed dead once before. The sunburnt skin suggestive of an outdoorsman — in this case, a mountain climber — underscores the point. Unhappily, on this occasion his death is more than mere presumption."

"My word. No sooner does one rejoice that the fellow has not died falling from some foreign peak than one discovers His Lordship has been murdered upon his return to London. Quite a horrific blow to the poor man's family."

"Ah," said Holmes, putting down his cup. "You did not read to the end of the story. If you had, not only would you have learned that the older brother had taken rooms at Walsingham House, but also that Howell Ingraham, the Earl's father and only surviving parent, is gravely ill. In fact, as of yesterday, the Marquis of Putnam was not expected to live through the night. What his condition is today one can only speculate."

I shook my head in disbelief: two tragedies for a noble family. And yet one could also not discount the other body we had discovered in the Boston Street house. "And the dead woman," I asked, "was there anything in the newspaper about her?"

"Not in the daily prints, old fellow. The report of the double murders has yet to appear. But realising that I still had time to look round the place before the police arrived, I was able to thumb through some letters I found in the library. Although I discovered nothing of value, I did manage to confirm that the young woman in question was indeed the Russian called Natasha Tamarova."

"Just as Davis said — though the name means nothing to me."

With a laconic smile, Holmes walked over to the sofa upon which lay one of his indexes, those large commonplace books he regularly filled with newspaper cuttings about contemporary figures to be found on either side of the law. He had obviously been studying it before I came down for breakfast.

Opening wide the large, brown, pasteboard covers, he carefully turned the pages made stiff with the glue he had used to affix his various cuttings. When he found what he was looking for, he brought the book to the table for me to view.

Though missing an illustration, a brief newspaper story told of a notorious young Russian woman born in St Petersburg who had come to England at an early age and currently lived in Boston Street. She was known for her escapades with various men of wealth.

"If I understand what you are saying, Holmes, the Earl of Ingraham returned home on Friday; and yesterday he and a Russian adventuress with whom he had shared some part of the evening were both stabbed to death."

"Quite so, Watson," said Holmes as he resumed his seat at the table. "Yet there is much more to learn. Though we have named the deceased, two significant mysteries in addition to the identity of the killer still remain — the discovery of whoever hurried past us on his way out of No. 11 Boston Street last night and the whereabouts of the butler who also fled the scene."

Suddenly, I put down my bread. The danger in which we had inadvertently placed ourselves the previous night now permeated my brain. "Why, that unknown man who rushed out the gate might have been the killer himself."

"He probably was," said Holmes as he calmly drank more coffee. "There is also an additional question. What, if anything, does the murder of a Russian adventuress have to do with Richard Harding Davis and the necklace he was transporting? Someone in the Ingraham family may know the answer. There remain the dead man's younger brother, and his elderly father, Lord Putnam, who, as you just heard, is deathly ill."

"I should think we must visit His Lordship as soon as possible then, whilst — or if — he is still able to speak to us."

"Agreed, old fellow. Conveniently, he lives close by — in Ulster Terrace in the Outer Circle Road. It is a walk of but a few minutes."

iii

The Outer Circle Road runs round the nearby Regent's Park. Had we made the journey on foot in the debilitating fog of the night before, it would have taken us hours. Today, however, beneath a bright, late-morning sun in the brisk December air, we arrived within fifteen minutes. Even so, the police were already there. For some reason, a Black Maria with its small, barred windows was positioned before the stately London home of the Marquis of Putnam.

The house itself, situated just west of Park Square, faces the south side of Regent's Park. One in a series of connected homes designed by John Nash, it stands three storeys tall, and the near-cylindrical western-most corner of each floor features a pair of curved bow windows. With their broad slate roofs, chalk-white stucco walls, semi-circular arches, Ionic colonnades, and intricate cornices, none of the distinguished homes leave any doubt concerning the wealth of their owners.

"Shall we?" said Holmes, indicating the flags that led to the entrance.

Before we had taken two steps towards the house, however, the japanned outer door opened, and a gentleman exited. He was placing a trilby on his head as we passed; and with his long, dark coat hanging open, I could not help noticing a handsome, black-pearl stud in the middle of his shirt-front. His curling moustache merely confirmed for me that here was the same man who had raised Davis' suspicions in the High Table when the disposition of the Queen's necklace had been discussed.

"You're wasting your time," he muttered cryptically.

But neither Holmes nor I had the chance to respond, for Lord Putnam's silver-haired butler stood framed in the portal holding the door open for us.

"Who was that man who just left?" Holmes asked when we reached entrance.

The butler looked us over before answering. "Are you referring to Sir Roderick Childs, sir?" he responded coldly.

"Indeed," said Holmes, casting a knowing look in my direction.

We all stood staring at one another for an awkward moment. Finally, Holmes said, "We're here to see Lord Putnam."

"Follow me," the butler intoned. Saying nothing more, he led us through the broad foyer, past various servants in their plush livery, and into a large sitting room filled with fine furniture, rich wall-hangings, and lots of brass fittings.

There was no sign of the ailing Marquis, but that sad omission did not mean the room was unoccupied. The small, lean form of the sitting room's solitary inhabitant rose from a stiff-backed wing chair. Facing us was Inspector Lestrade.

Holmes and I recognised the look of curious surprise with which Lestrade greeted us. It was the same expression we had seen on the previous occasions we magically seemed to materialise at the scene of some unpublicised crime. It began suspiciously enough with raised eyebrows and narrowing dark eyes but slowly devolved into a smile of resignation, the same sort of sheepish grin one displays when encountering something which appears beyond one's understanding.

"How you got here so quickly, gentlemen," observed the Inspector a bit too loudly, "I'm sure I'll never know. But I'm assuming, Mr. Holmes, you deduced that the dead man you found in the house in Boston Street last night was Lord

Putnam's heir, the Earl of Ingraham, fresh back from South America."

"A truly sad state of affairs," I offered.

"You're right there, Doctor," said Lestrade shaking his head. "Thought to be dead; then resurrected; now dead again."

"Have you spoken to the Marquis about all that has happened?" Holmes asked. "I understand he is quite ill."

The policeman rocked back and forth. "We tried talking to him, Mr. Holmes, but His Lordship is drugged or hallucinating or sleeping. Or all three. At any rate, we could not get him to understand. Perhaps you saw the Baronet who just left—Sir Roderick Childs. A Member of Parliament, he is, and couldn't get a word in."

"What about the younger son then?" I asked.

"That's a bit delicate, I'm afraid," said the Inspector, wrinkling his nose. "You see, Lord Cyril is nowhere to be found. In point of fact, we came here tonight for two reasons — not only to inform the Marquis of the death of his immediate heir; but also — " here he cleared his throat — "to arrest Lord Cyril Ingraham for the two murders in Boston Street."

"Brother killing brother?" I scoffed. "Like Cain and Abel? Surely, Lestrade, you can't be serious."

"Quite serious, Doctor. We've made enquiries, you see. We've been following the activities of young Cyril, the new Earl of Ingraham, for quite a while now — actually, ever since the older brother went missing some months ago. It was good, old-fashioned coppering if I do say so myself."

Holmes furrowed his brow. "Just what have you learned?"

The policeman drew a small notebook from his coat pocket and flipped through the pages till he found the relevant section. "It seems," said he, looking down at his cribbed writing, "that when the original heir went missing, the younger son, assuming himself to be the new heir, began upping his expenditures.

"New clothes from Bond Street, late-night parties in restaurants and saloons, and lots of money devoted to games of chance." Lestrade turned to the next page. "In fact, he's become a regular, if unlucky, patron of the Tankerville Club, where he has — according to what others have told us — gone heavily into debt."

I surveyed the lavish furnishings that surrounded us — the silver candelabras, the distinguished portraits, the Waterford crystal. "Believing himself to be the rightful heir to all this," said I, waving my arms about expansively, "and his father so ill — one can readily understand why the young man might throw caution to the wind."

"And yet," added Holmes, "a plan completely upended by the re-appearance of the missing older brother."

"My point exactly, Mr. Holmes," said Lestrade. "Within the single day of his brother's return, the younger man discovered that his own life had become a nightmare. It is our theory at the Yard that upon hearing of his older brother's resurrection, Lord Cyril realised he had lost his pipeline to the funds that were keeping the moneylenders at bay. Killing his brother remained the only viable solution to his financial problems."

However distasteful Lestrade's hypothesis, one could not deny its possibility. The younger son's debts clearly established a motive for terminating the true heir's return. Yet with the ailing Marquis unresponsive and the new Earl of Ingraham not at home, there seemed little reason for any of us to remain in their house.

Lestrade agreed. "I was hoping Lord Putnam might come round," observed the Inspector. "But since he hasn't, I don't fancy spending any more of my time in this place." With a pull of the bell cord, he rang for the butler who escorted us to the door.

Dark clouds were scudding across a hazy afternoon sky as Lestrade climbed into the police van. Holmes and I hurried back to Baker Street on foot, hoping to avoid the rain.

iv

An hour after we arrived at our rooms, Billy knocked at the door. He carried with him a message from Lestrade. *Lord Cyril Ingraham injured in accident last night,* it read. *Found today in Bart's Common Ward. Meet me there at 2 o'clock.*

Once Holmes had shown me the Inspector's communication, he was already donning his cape and travelling cap. "Come, Watson! We have less than a quarter hour. Let us be off."

Full of questions, I grabbed my long coat and bowler and eagerly followed.

No sooner did we reach the sidewalk than we discovered that the threat of rain had turned to reality. With the angry heavens letting loose a great downpour, it was from under an awning that Holmes hailed a passing hansom. "St. Bartholomew's Hospital!" he shouted up to the driver, and bravely dodging the raindrops, we climbed into the cab. "Quickly, man!"

Before we were even in our seats, the hansom lunged forward. A long peal of thunder covered the clatter of the horse's hooves as we sped dangerously down a drenched Baker Street and then swung eastward into the equally sodden Marylebone Road.

Chapter Four

St. Bart's

The secret of good writing
is to say an old thing in a new way
or to say a new thing in an old way.
— Richard Harding Davis
attr.

i

The heavy rain continued to splash about us as Holmes and I bolted from hansom to hospital. In fact, we entered through the same side door of St. Bart's that I remembered using in '81 on the day Holmes and I had first met. We climbed the same stone staircase as well. When we reached the second storey on this occasion, however, we strode down the long corridor that led *away* from the chemical laboratory where my dresser Stamford had introduced us.

Still, the hallway in which we now found ourselves featured the same whitewashed walls, dun-coloured doors, and low-arched ceilings that I remembered from the day of our meeting. This corridor, however, delivered us not to the labs but to the double-doors of the common ward where we found Lestrade waiting for us in front of a uniformed constable.

Through the large windows set in the doors behind the policeman I could see the rows of iron-railed hospital beds and all manner of prostrate occupants. In various positions of ailment, they were being ministered to by a handful of white-coated doctors, dressers and nurses.

"Over there," Lestrade indicated with the jerk of his head towards the back of the ward.

Difficult as it was to believe, in a bed against the dun-coloured far wall of the common ward, a white, turban-like bandage encircling his brow, lay His Lordship, Cyril Ingraham, the new heir to the Marquis of Putnam.

Unable to mask my surprise, I cried out, "Do you mean to say, Inspector, that the heir to Lord Putnam is being treated in the same ward as the sick and impoverished?"

I had reason to be shocked. As my faithful readers will recall, before joining the Army Hospital Corps at Netley, I had taken my Doctor of Medicine degree at the University of London. As a University hospital, Bart's was my *alma mater*; and I had learned its procedures well. In particular, I knew that when forced to be in hospital at all, the exalted members of London society did not share rooms with the *hoi polloi*.

"Now, now, Doctor," the Inspector said, raising his hands to calm me down. "You must recall that no one knew the man's identity at first. Brought in unconscious with a head wound, he was. Seems to have suffered a concussion.

According to the reports, Cyril Ingraham is lucky to be alive."

"Precisely, what happened?" Holmes wanted to know.

"Here's what I've been told," offered Lestrade. "It had just gone six when he was seen coming out of Walsingham House."

"Yes, we know — " I was about to add that, owing to the note Holmes had seen, we also were aware that the older brother had requested Lord Cyril to meet him there. Holmes, however, touched my arm to silence me.

"Moments later," continued Lestrade, the man was run down in the fog by a four-wheeler. When he finally did come round earlier this afternoon and explained who he was, the doctors decided it was safer to leave him in the ward than move him to private quarters."

As Lestrade spoke, I thought I heard the echo of muffled footfalls coming down the corridor Holmes and I had just traversed, as if someone might have been following us on tiptoe. Of course, the steps could have belonged to anyone who worked in the place; but then, strangely, just as they had increased in volume, so did they just as quickly diminish and disappear.

"The constable, Lestrade?" I asked, having decided to redirect my worries from imagined footfalls to the patient's well-being. "Is *he* necessary for the young man's health as well?"

The Inspector sighed. "I know you're thinking like the medical man you are, Doctor; but injured or not, we can't have Lord Cyril running off just now, can we? Lest you forget, regardless of his condition, he remains a murder suspect. Our man here is one of a rotating shift."

I shook my head. "Look at the poor fellow! Anyone can see that he appears sufficiently incapacitated not to entertain any idea of escape."

Holmes now entered the fray. "With the fog we had last night, Lestrade, if it were late afternoon that he was injured, then he could not possibly have got to Boston Street from Walsingham House in time to commit those murders."

"What Holmes is suggesting," I explained to the Inspector, "is that the bandaged fellow we have come here to see may be totally innocent."

Lestrade shook his head. "Who knows? Maybe he done the murders earlier than we thought. Or maybe he had them arranged. There's no denying that possibility, eh, Mr. Holmes?"

"Perhaps not. But what if Lord Cyril's unfortunate encounter with the carriage was no accident? He might still be danger. In which case, Lestrade, no matter your intention, the sentry you've posted may be serving more as protector than jailer."

Lestrade shrugged. "I take your point, Mr. Holmes. In any case, given your interest in this nasty business, I thought you gentlemen might like to be in attendance when we hear his story. Perhaps it will address the very issues you have mentioned."

"Perhaps," repeated Holmes, "though I doubt the matter is as simple as that."

The bitter-sweet tang of sickness and carbolic immediately overwhelmed us as soon as Lestrade pushed open the doors to the common ward. Inhaling as little as possible, the three of us marched determinedly towards Lord Cyril's hospital bed, the echoes of our footfalls mingling with the moans and groans of the ill.

His Lordship looked to be in his early twenties; but with his bandaged brow and dark-circled eyes, the age of the stricken patient remained hard to determine. And yet however ghoulish his appearance, I could not fail to note the resemblance between the sharpness of Lord Cyril's features and those of his murdered brother. One might easily have mistaken one for the other.

A uniformed nurse attired in white cap, white apron, and long-sleeved black dress stood at attention by his bedside. She quavered not at all as the small army of men approached her station.

"Police business," Lestrade announced.

Lord Cyril's eyes immediately focused on the Inspector.

"This patient is *my* business," the nurse replied calmly. "Doctor told me to expect you, but that does not mean I will allow you to do His Lordship any harm. I shall remain a few feet away and intercede if you upset him."

She checked a small silver watch pinned to the bib of her white apron. "Five minutes, *gentlemen.*" She pronounced this last word as if it were a compliment she was compelled to employ by reason of *her* own august position, not that of Scotland Yard.

"*Upset* him?" Lestrade growled. "Of course, I'm going to upset him. I'm going to question him concerning his brother's murder."

The nurse offered no reaction to these last words; but upon hearing them spoken, Lord Cyril attempted to sit up. As soon as he tried to move, however, he grimaced in pain and fell back onto his pillow. "*Murder?*" he managed to spit out. "My brother isn't dead. Don't you know? He's just returned from South America. I saw him yesterday." With a slight tilt of his head, he added, "At least, I think it was yesterday."

"You *think* it was yesterday," Lestrade parroted derisively.

It required but an instant for Holmes to touch the Inspector's arm and urge him away from the bed. At first, I thought Holmes was about to inform Lestrade of the note in the dead man's pocket that confirmed Lord Cyril's account of the meeting. What I actually heard was an appeal for discretion. "A bit of prudence might be in order, Lestrade," Holmes was saying quietly. "Perhaps you should listen to the young man's story before putting the manacles on him."

"Here now, Mr. Holmes, just what did you expect him to say — '*I done it!*' — just like that?"

"I am not one to tell Scotland Yard how to perform their duties," Holmes whispered, "but you don't want to go about accusing the wrong person, especially not someone of his rank. Remember that Lord Cyril was placed in this common ward only because no one knew his true identity when he was brought in. Do not forget whom you are interrogating, Lestrade. With his brother's death, he is now the new Earl of Ingraham and heir to the Marquis of Putnam." Holmes raised his bushy eyebrows in hopes of encouraging Lestrade not to make a monumental error.

The Inspector stroked his chin for a moment. "I take your meaning, Mr. Holmes," he said at last. "Indeed, I do. Let's hear him out then." As Lestrade moved back towards the patient, he turned round, placed a forefinger to his lips and whispered to us, "Caution's the word."

"First, Inspector," said Holmes as we returned to the side of the bed, "you must introduce us."

Lestrade cleared his throat. Then he announced each of our names, including his own; and Holmes and I dipped our heads to the new Earl by way of salutation.

All the while, the nurse stood in the background, arms folded across her chest, nodding in approval at the now more even-tempered tone of Lestrade's opening remarks. Nonetheless, she continued to keep her lips pressed tightly together in preparation for a speech of reprimand should Lestrade provide her reason to employ it.

A few moments of uncertain silence passed before Holmes said, "You must inform His Lordship about what happened last night."

"What — what *did* happen last night?" a bewildered Lord Cyril asked.

"Yes," Lestrade muttered, more to himself than to anyone else. Then he said, "Let me begin, Your Lordship by saying that I am truly sorry to have to inform you that your brother, Rochester Ingraham, formerly the Earl of Ingraham, was found murdered last night in a house in Boston Street."

The new Earl shook his head. "Chet? Murdered? No. That's impossible. He only just arrived back in England. You must be mistaken. How — how can that be? I already told you — I saw him last evening. I remember now. That blasted fog. I must have been on my way back from visiting him when they tell me I was run over by a carriage."

"Where was it that you last saw him?" Lestrade asked. "And what time was it — do you recall?"

"Why, in — in his rooms at Walsingham House. It must have been sometime after five."

"We estimate that his death occurred not long thereafter." Lestrade proceeded to describe the murder scene to the young man — how Holmes and I had found his brother stabbed to death in the house in Boston Street and how a young Russian woman had been killed there as well.

"A *Russian* woman!" Lord Cyril closed his eyes. "No! No! *No!*" he muttered, shaking his head back and forth.

The nurse stepped forward, but Holmes intervened. "This man is a doctor," he said, pointing at me.

I nodded, but she cast a sceptical eye my way. She did take a step back, however, and allowed Holmes to proceed.

"Pray, my Lord," said he, "tell us anything you might know of this matter. We don't want to wait for the inquest to begin our investigation."

The patient tried once more to sit up. I helped him prop his flimsy pillow against the head-rail, and eventually he managed to settle himself in an upright position.

It must have been a full minute that he sat silently with his head down. In the quiet we could hear the rain drumming against the windows, its constant rattle helping conceal the cries of the poor souls elsewhere in the ward.

When the Earl looked up, his expression was bleak. "On Saturday," he said, "I learned from the public prints that my brother lived — that he had *not* died in a horrible mountain accident some months ago, but rather that he had arrived from South America the day before and that he was staying at Walsingham House. As you can imagine, I was overjoyed at the news and immediately sent him good wishes. We exchanged notes agreeing on a time to meet later that afternoon, and I went to see him."

"Instead of taking rooms at a hotel," Lestrade wanted to know, "why did your brother not go directly home?"

"He and my father do not get along, Inspector. They'd had a serious row concerning the young woman that my father correctly believed Chet was spending time with."

"The Russian?" I asked.

"Yes. The Russian. Apparently a common, seductive sort. The irony is that before he left for South America, Chet told me that he had broken off with her. But yesterday afternoon he confessed that she had written to him in Ecuador. She had said she was suffering from some sort of serious illness, and it was his concern for her that brought him back to England. Not that I think he really believed her, but he insisted he had to be certain."

"Your father's instincts about the woman were right then," I said.

"Yes, they probably were. But no matter the differences he had with my brother, it should have been our father's illness that brought Chet home, not some wild story fabricated by a Russian temptress in order to get him back."

I was pleased to hear Lord Ingraham voicing these words. I was confident the Marquis would appreciate such sentiments from his younger son.

"But, you see," the new Earl went on, a furrow creasing the line of forehead exposed below the white bandaging, "Chet had left me no way to contact him in South America, so he didn't know of our father's condition. There was every possibility that Father would not last the night; and fog or no fog, I had to inform my brother.

"Quite right," I said.

"When I broke the news to Chet at Walsingham House last evening, he said he would come to the house directly, but first he had to see the Russian woman. He swore that it would be the last time — that he planned to end it with her once for all. Then he sent me on my way. I left

76

Walsingham House just after six o'clock. That was when the hansom or the growler — whatever it was — ran me down."

"So, My Lord," Lestrade persisted, "you claim to know nothing about your brother's murder? Or the woman's?"

"*No,* I tell you." His voice sounded agitated, and I noted the nurse checking her watch again.

Holmes, observing her movement as well, asked his final question. "What do *you* think might have occurred then, Lord Ingraham?"

"I don't know what to think. Learning of my brother's death is just as shocking to me as waking up here in hospital. Maybe the Russian woman stabbed him when he told her their friendship was over. That *must* be it! Then she must have killed herself."

"We found no knife," said Lestrade. "If this really was a murder and a suicide, the knife would have been there in plain view."

"Nonetheless," murmured the Earl, "it must be so."

"She was stabbed in the heart," I said. "A frightening way to commit suicide, would you not agree?"

A sardonic smile crossed the young man's face. "It worked for Juliet," he said.

"But this lady who topped herself," offered Lestrade, missing the reference to Shakespeare, "was called Natasha."

"Look for the knife!" cried the young man. "I'm sure you'll find it, and it will prove my story."

"With respect, Lord Ingraham," countered Lestrade, "we know of your gambling problems. We know that with your brother previously thought to be dead in South America and your father on his death-bed here in London, you believed yourself about to become the new Marquis of Putnam and therefore able to pay off your debtors."

The Earl's eyes widened, as he sensed the accusation implicit in Lestrade's comments.

The Inspector now pointed a finger at His Lordship. "But your brother returned, didn't he? And you were suddenly faced with the sad fact that the credit you had planned to collect from the post obits was suddenly non-existent. You realised that your creditors would soon be coming after you. Eliminate your newly found brother, and you eliminate your financial problems."

"No!" exclaimed the Earl. "I was in the best of moods after speaking to Chet. Why should I not be? He was alive, he was planning to say good-bye to the Russian woman, and he was going to reconcile with Father. What could be better, Inspector? Look for the knife, I tell you! It will show you I had nothing to do with those murders. Not with either one!"

"Even if we did find a knife," Lestrade countered, "who's to say you didn't leave it there for us to discover?"

"No!" Lord Cyril shouted.

Following this last outburst, the nurse intervened. "That is quite enough. His Lordship needs rest." Unceremoniously waving us towards the exit, she said, "Please be so kind as to leave."

Lestrade's face reddened, and he took a deep breath to control his anger. "Lord Ingraham," said he, "you'll be hearing from us again. I have posted a constable at the door to be sure you don't decide to run off in the middle of the night the way you did from Walsingham House."

Holmes and I dipped our heads as we left, and the Earl slumped down in the bed again.

Once we reached the corridor, Lestrade turned to Holmes. "'Suicide!' he said with a laugh. "With a knife to the heart? Have you ever heard such humbug?"

"It is because the Earl's story *is* so much humbug," Holmes said grimly, "that I *do* believe it."

Lestrade's eyebrows shot up.

"Think, Lestrade. Why concoct a story whose credibility could be so easily undermined if the knife were missing? If Lord Cyril truly believes the knife is still there, then he must truly believe that the woman really did kill herself after stabbing his brother."

"So he says," offered Lestrade.

"But you found no such object. Nor did Watson or I. So unless some third party took it — the butler, perhaps, or more probably the killer (though they could be one and the same) — the theory of a double murder remains. No, Lestrade, the Earl's misguided faith in a murder-suicide plot helps to confirm his innocence."

The policeman scratched his head. "When you put it that way, Mr. Holmes, I reckon you may have a point. And yet the motive for the Earl still remains — a way out from under all that debt."

Lestrade too had scored a legitimate point. Clearly, there were questions that needed answering. The butler from Boston Street, for one, still remained missing. He represented a loose strand in the story that, if pulled upon, might yield worthy results.

"I'm off to the Yard," said Lestrade. "But first let us agree to share whatever additional information we might secure."

"Agreed," answered Holmes with a nod.

I followed my friend to the stairs, and the two of us made our way out to the street through the same corridors we had traversed on our way in.

iii

The rain had stopped by the time we left St. Bart's. It was late afternoon; and as Holmes hailed a hansom, the lights of the city were already reflecting madly off water-laden King Edward Street.

"What of Davis?" I asked once we had climbed into the cab. "You told him you would be talking with him today. We must inform him of what we have just learned from the Earl."

"Quite so, Watson," Holmes murmured without much interest.

"Now that the weather has cleared," I persisted, "we should stop in at Davis' hotel and tell him all that has transpired."

"Why don't *you* see to it, old fellow? I have other matters of concern." Tapping his breast pocket, he explained, "I shall go to Whitehall. It is time I gave this necklace back to Mycroft."

"Holmes!" I cried, having had no idea that he was so cavalierly carrying a diamond necklace on his person. Immediately, I looked round the interior of the hansom and out its windows. Who knew what sort of thieves might be following us?

All I succeeded in accomplishing, however, was to evoke a dry chuckle from my friend. "I should imagine that Mycroft will have to make new plans for delivering the bauble to Lady Brownlow — though I do believe he still has time to get it to her before Christmas. Besides, there are some other matters I need to discuss with him. Allow me to inform the driver of your destination." Leaning out the window, he shouted up, "155 Piccadilly! The Bath Hotel."

iv

I climbed out of the hansom beneath the imposing eight storeys of the red-bricked Walsingham House, the hostelry in which the elder Ingraham brother had spent the final two days of his life. As I approached my true destination, the more modest Bath next door, a flurry of activity illuminated by the gas lamps at its entrance attracted my attention.

As luck would have it, at the very moment of my arrival Richard Harding Davis in long coat and tall hat was stepping out for the evening. Fluttering on each of his arms was a handsome young woman attired in dark wool cape and sable collar. One of the charmers looked surprisingly familiar.

"Ah, Dr. Watson," cried Davis. "You just caught me. Actually, I was on my way to the theatre with my friends. May I introduce you?"

I immediately removed my bowler.

"This delightful creature," said Davis with a tilt of his head to the woman on his right, "is my old friend, Miss Ethel Barrymore, the American actress. I call her the Duchess."

The broad-nosed beauty smiled in my direction. "*Long-time* friend, Dick, not '*old*'," she corrected.

"Of course," said Davis and patted her hand apologetically. "Rude on my part. Mother brought me up to be better than that." Then he tilted his head to the left. "And this lovely lady, Doctor, is a product of your very own British stage, Miss Cissie Loftus."

Ah, yes, the woman I had recognised. The Barrymore name I knew only by reputation; the family were famous for their theatrical accomplishments both in America and here in England. Cissie Loftus, on the other hand, I had seen in the flesh, as it were, in London music halls.

During my younger years, groups of us medical students would escape from our tedious work at Bart's in search of relaxation. And what better diversion could one find than the wild entertainment provided by the clever comics, confounding magicians, and beautiful women who performed under the watchful eye of the "Chairman," the master of ceremonies for the theatrical proceedings?[6]

As I grew older, of course, my interest in such trivialities dissipated. Upon becoming a physician, an author, and later a husband, I found myself consumed by new responsibilities. But eventually there came not only the death of my dear wife Mary; but also what I, along with the rest of the world, presumed to be the demise of Sherlock Holmes at the hands of Professor Moriarty.

To minimise the emptiness, the desolation, the pain, I initially felt when Mary died, I occupied myself with medical work and the investigations I shared with Holmes. But when I thought I had lost my friend and colleague as well?

I have already written of my activities during the three years prior to Holmes' resurrection — how I buried myself in my surgery and how I contributed my practical knowledge to cases for Scotland Yard. But there remains more to tell as seeing Cissie Loftus that evening suggested.

Devastated by the losses of those closest to me, I discovered that distracting habits are difficult to break — especially those cultivated during one's youth. In addition

---

[6] For some insights into Dr. Watson's experiences with London music halls, see Michael Hardwick's *The Private Life of Dr. Watson: Being the Reminiscences of John H. Watson, M.D.* (DDV)

to the aforementioned altruism I displayed during the extended period of my grief, I owe it to my faithful readers to recount the madcap hours I also spent renewing my proclivity for the music halls of London.

In such theatres as the Oxford, the Tivoli and the Canterbury, performers like the diminutive comedian and singer Dan Leno and the even smaller Little Tich with his outrageous big-boot dance served as welcome antidotes to my grief. Thus, it should not come as a surprise for readers to learn that in July of '93, I happened to be seated in the Oxford when the charming Miss Loftus made her stage debut.

Oh, I could mention her delightful voice and uncanny ability to mimic other singers of the day — the daring French *chanteuse* Yvette Guilbert comes to mind. But then I would be ignoring what enables me to envision Cissie's performance to this very day — those large, mournful eyes so at odds with the sprightly nature of her act. They reminded me of Mary in '93 even as they did now staring up at me as part of the young woman's warm smile.

"Dr. John Watson," I said, reinserting myself into reality. "I have had the pleasure of seeing you on the stage, Miss Loftus."

She responded with a coquettish blush, and amidst the chorus of giggling emitted by both ladies, Davis leaned towards me. "What was it you wanted to see me about, Doctor?" he asked. "Something to do with the *murders*?" This last word he voiced in a stage whisper, ostensibly not to be overheard. In reality, he might just as well have shouted it. If holding the women's interest had been his purpose, he had succeeded masterfully.

Indeed, upon Davis' utterance of the word, the women stifled their laughter, obviously eager to hear some morsel of whatever ghoulish detail must have brought me round to Davis' hotel. As tempting as it was to capture the full attention of these beauties, however, I reasoned that a report on Lord Ingraham in hospital or the latest developments concerning the murdered pair in Boston Street was not to be shared with the ladies.

"Another time," I said as I watched the women turn their heads from me in disappointment. "I hope you enjoy your evening."

With those words, I replaced my bowler and, savouring my memory of Cissie Loftus' soulful eyes, turned north in Piccadilly. Behind me, I heard Miss Barrymore say, "Let's walk, Duke," and Davis reply with a laugh, "Whatever you say, Duchess."

Turning round to look, I saw the trio marching off in the direction of Drury Lane.

Chapter Five

Thuggery

To my dear friend [actor] Henry E. Dixey
whose make-up . . . I copied and whose suggestion
I followed when I spent a week among
the "confiding crooks of Wood Street."
— Richard Harding Davis
Inscribed on the back of a Photo
of himself
The Bookman, June 1916

i

As I had hoped, the visit to my surgery the next morning, a chill Monday, lasted less than an hour. The short work-period left me the rest of the day to help Holmes resolve the Boston Street murders. With no one waiting to see me after I had administered to the only two patients who had come in — abrasions bothered one; an annoying cough irritated the other — I felt comfortable locking the door and returning to our rooms. Happily, no other medical issues were raising cause for alarm.

Would the same could be said for conditions at Baker Street. As soon as I alighted from my hansom at 221, I noted an unsavoury fellow loitering across the road. He was leaning against the wall of the yellow brick building opposite our windows. To conceal his face, he had pulled a flat cap over his brow and turned up the collar of his heavy dark coat. And yet I could still discern the stubble on his chin and an unlit cigar butt at his lips. Worse, from the direction of his gaze, I saw that he was clearly watching our rooms.

I hurried up the stairs to inform Sherlock Holmes. "There's a sinister-looking character eying our windows from across the road," I announced upon entering the sitting room.

My friend rose from the table where he had been enjoying a cup of tea. Slowly, he walked to the window, calmly pushed aside the white curtain, and casually glanced outside.

"Yes, Watson. I noticed him earlier."

"But shouldn't we worry? The blackguard seems to be focusing on *our* rooms in particular. He might mean us harm. At the very least, he could frighten off your clients — not to mention distressing Mrs. Hudson."

Holmes dismissed my concern with the wave of his hand. "More important at the moment, old fellow, is what I learned earlier this morning. I too was out. I visited the Public Record Office in Chancery Lane with the intention of discovering who owns No. 11 Boston Street."

"An excellent idea, Holmes, but — "

"Yes, I know. You're worried about the stranger across the road. Trust me — the fact that those papers could not be located is more significant than that — what did you call him? — 'sinister-looking character' outside our windows. I tell you, Watson, only someone with connections to the government could have had a hand in removing those papers."

Significant indeed — Lieutenant Stanton and the MP, Sir Roderick Childs, came to mind — but I would not be put off. "The man outside," I reminded him.

"Yes, yes," Holmes sighed, casting a lingering look at the fire, "Very well then. Let's have a talk with this miscreant who has so disturbed you."

Holmes' tepid call to action made me feel as if the alarm I had sounded concerned only myself. Indeed, Holmes appeared not at all distressed. He did not even bother to don his coat as he left the sitting room. In point of fact, I thought I detected a glimmer of amusement in his grey eyes as he confronted the cold in his shirtsleeves.

Dodging the carriages and hansoms clattering along Baker Street, Holmes made his way across the road in the direction of the stranger. I did my best to follow.

The nearer Holmes got to the surly looking fellow, the more the vagrant pulled at his coat collar to engulf most all of his lower face. The little I could spy of his expression turned even more sullen as Holmes approached him. I thought it wiser for my friend to keep his distance until he had a greater opportunity to take the measure of the man.

Pulling down the bill of his cap, the rogue greeted Holmes with a grunt.

"A member of the Players' Club, I presume," my friend muttered cryptically.

"What's that, Holmes?" I asked from behind.

"You know the old saying, Watson: 'A thief knows a thief as well as a wolf knows a wolf.' Only in this case, we're speaking of actors. I too have been on the stage." As he spoke, he moved closer to the menacing figure. "Isn't that right, Mr. Davis? I recognised you the first time I noticed you from our window."

Only then did I too penetrate the disguise. This stubble-chinned roughneck was the same man I had seen the night before with a woman on each arm. Today he was arrayed in make-up and costume — sans walking stick, I might add.

"Here then," I demanded. "What's all this about?"

"Inside," commanded Holmes.

Davis threw his cigar butt to the kerb in obvious annoyance at being recognised. Then the three of us negotiated the harrowing trek back across the road and up the seventeen steps to our sitting room where it was decidedly warmer.

Whilst Davis and I removed our coats, Holmes headed for his armchair by the fire. Davis settled into a nearby chair; and before joining them, I poured each of us a cup of the remaining tea.

"Now then, Mr. Davis," said I, the one gulled by his disguise, "explain yourself."

The fearsome expression metamorphosed into a broad smile. "To get a story some ten years ago for the *Philadelphia Press,*" Davis said, "I adopted the guise of a no-account so I could infiltrate a gang of thieves.

"With the aid of some make-up sticks and powder and a vagrant's costume from a play called *The Romany Eye,* I looked like the real thing. Called myself 'Buck' Meiley out of New York. Not only did the episode provide me good material to write about, but I also managed to alert the police to some evil goings-on."

Bravely done! I may have been duped by Davis' performance; but as a writer who sometimes exposed my own person to danger, I could well applaud the risks taken by a dedicated pressman. "Good show," I said to him. "But Holmes mentioned the Players."

"An association of theatre people in New York. I am indeed a member," Davis boasted. "It was organised in Gramercy Park by the late, great actor Edwin Booth."

"The brother of Lincoln's assassin," I said.

"The same — though we didn't speak of it much. Booth knew my work — my scribblings about the theatre, even some of my acting. And I've already told you that I've been writing a script based on *Soldiers of Fortune.* So, you see, I come by this theatrical get-up quite honestly."

"Most admirable," I said.

"And now," said Holmes, "to the larger question: what sort of game is afoot? Why are you in disguise?"

Davis clapped his hands in tribute to his success. "I was being an amateur detective, Mr. Holmes. I found myself wondering what might have happened to the Boston Street butler; and I concluded that since he had run off from the house so quickly the other night, he just might have some reason for returning there as well."

"A shot in the dark," I mused. "And a dangerous one at that."

"But a keen one nonetheless," said Davis obviously proud of his insight, "for the fellow did indeed come back."

Holmes leaned forward. "Even with the constable that Lestrade has posted at the outer door? There's been a policeman on duty at No. 11 for the past two days."

Davis smiled, his lantern jaw jutting upward. "Naturally, I figured the police would be there—that's why I decided to wear a disguise. I'm quite convinced that my customary attire would attract attention."

"To be sure," said I, thinking of the fur-lined frock coat, the putative medals, the ebony walking stick.

"It was easy to pick up some old clothes at the street market near my hotel—and then go loiter near the house. I can assure you that it was much easier to find in the light of day than in that miserable fog of Saturday night."

"And what exactly did you learn, Mr. Davis?" Holmes asked with that familiar glint of anticipation in his steel-grey eyes.

Davis rubbed his hands together at the enjoyment of becoming the cynosure once again. "First," he began dramatically, "I crossed the road. Then I positioned myself behind some shade trees where I couldn't be seen and made myself comfortable. Who knew how long I'd have to be out there?"

"And?" Holmes encouraged him.

"As luck would have it, I didn't have long to wait. For soon enough I saw the butler return. Now here's the strange part, gentlemen. Like me, he too hid behind some trees — but whereas I was across the street, he remained on the same side as the house — in the shadows, but near the house none the less. What's more, the fellow peered around a lot — like maybe he was expecting someone and fearful of being surprised."

"Understandably so," said I. "He must realise that the police are searching for him. And then there's that constable posted at the door."

"True," Davis agreed, "but mostly the fellow faced east — away from the house — and he frequently checked his watch. It was as if he had some sort of *rendezvous* at a certain time."

"Anyone could have been coming to meet him," I observed

"Agreed, Watson," said Holmes. "Yet Davis is right to suggest that the butler was putting himself in danger by returning to No. 11. He could have met the mysterious party elsewhere. No, there is something singularly magnetic about that house in Boston Street."

Davis raised a hand to stop Holmes' line of enquiry. "No need to speculate, Mr. Holmes; I have the answer. He was waiting for the post."

"The post!" Holmes repeated. Now it was his turn to clap his hands. "Of course."

"I watched the postman in his grey flannel uniform and round, grey cap delivering the mail to all the houses on Boston Street," Davis said. "After a while, I saw him approaching No. 11.

"Before he could get there, however, he was accosted by the butler. The butler did a lot of shouting, which immediately attracted the attention of the constable at the front door. I could hear the word 'letter' bandied about, but the postman kept shaking his head. If I had to guess, I'd say that the butler was demanding the mail for the house — a letter of some sort. He couldn't very well go inside to collect it with the policeman guarding the front of the place."

Holmes nodded. "Even with a key to the rear entrance, it would have been too risky with a constable standing on the other side of the mail slot."

"So you can see his problem, gentlemen," offered Davis. "He wanted a letter, and the postman was refusing to give it to him."

"Hear, hear—for the Royal Mail," I said.

"When the postman did reach No. 11, he tipped his hat to the constable, slipped an envelope through the brass mail slot at the centre of the door, and continued on his rounds."

"And the butler?" Holmes asked.

"Oh, as soon as he saw the constable make a move in his direction, he stalked off angrily down the road in the direction of the Park. That was about an hour ago. That's also when I decided to come here. Your boy told me the two of you were out. To be fair," Davis chuckled, "he did look me over once or twice — you know, dressed the way I am."

I nodded in sympathy. "He's used to all sorts coming here to see Sherlock Holmes."

"Well, I waited across the road until I was sure you were both upstairs. I saw *you* arrive first, Mr. Holmes, and then you, Doctor. I was just about to go up to report all this to you when the two of you came out. Call me vain, Mr. Holmes, but I decided to maintain my disguise to see if I could fool a master detective like yourself. I guess I know the answer."

"Setting aside the quality of your costume," said my friend, refusing to be drawn into judging, "I would say that, overall, you've done very well. Now we must return to Boston Street and find a way into that house to see if we can lay our hands on the incriminating evidence."

"What incriminating evidence?" Davis asked.

"Why," answered Holmes, "whatever the butler was waiting for in the post."

We donned our long coats, and Holmes informed Billy that if any important messages should arrive, he could find us in the vicinity of No. 11, Boston Street. Then Davis, Holmes and I began to retrace our steps of Saturday night. I might add that Davis' sciatica must have been in abeyance, for he had little trouble walking without his cane. When his minor limp finally did manifest itself, his altered gait seemed merely part of his disguise.

We set out in the crisp, cool air beneath the late-morning sun. With no fog to hamper our progress, it required but a matter of minutes to reach Boston Street — time enough for Holmes to inform Davis of what we had learned since the three of us had discovered the bodies two nights before. In particular, Holmes reported to him the identities of the victims, the relationship between them, and Lord Cyril's situation in hospital.

Holmes completed his account just as we reached our destination. On this occasion, however, rather than heading for the front of No. 11, Holmes led Davis and me into the utilitarian alleyway that ran behind the string of terraced houses.

It was amidst full trash bins and pools of spent, soapy water that we eventually located the steps leading down to the weathered rear door of No. 11. A quick check revealed it to be locked; and Holmes immediately withdrew his tiny picks from inside a deep pocket, deftly unlatched the lock, and opened the door.

"Remember," he whispered with a forefinger to his lips, "we are here for the latest post. Do not forget the policeman at the front door."

That said, Holmes conducted us on tiptoe through a narrow, whitewashed corridor leading first to the kitchen and then on to the darkened rooms within the house's interior.

During this illegal entry, Holmes raised no questions about Davis' willingness to trespass. All three of us had already committed that crime on the night of the murders.

Fortunately, as we moved towards the entrance hall, we were able to avoid the rooms in which we had found the two bodies. Today we sought only the wooden post-box mounted on the inside of the front door—the same wooden post box, I just then remembered, that I had run into upon entering the house in the fog two nights before; the same wooden post box, I also just remembered, that had so curiously employed a lock.

A furrow of concern darkened Holmes' brow as soon as he saw the lock in question. "The butler must have the key," he said softly. "No doubt, to prevent the woman from seeing any correspondence not intended for her."

It goes without saying that neither the tiny brass lock nor the box itself represented much of an impediment to accessing the contents within. Holmes' delicate picks could easily handle the job. At the same time, one could not ignore the presence of the constable who stood so close on the other side of the door that through the fanlight we could discern the ridged rear-spine and silver-bossed top of his tall, black helmet.

Positioned as he was directly in front of the mail slot, the policeman could not possibly fail to hear any stray sounds emanating from within the supposedly empty house. Such sounds would, of course, include the picking of the lock.

Holmes tapped the American's arm. "Davis," he said in a hushed voice, "an opportunity has presented itself that will test your mettle as an actor."

In the sun pouring through the fanlight, one could immediately see Davis' face light up. "What is it, Mr. Holmes?"

"Go round to the front of the house and create a diversion, something that will require the policeman to leave his post and allow us the chance to make a modicum of noise in here."

"Right you are," whispered Davis with a smile and a mock-humble tug at his forelock. "I know just the thing." Then he turned and quietly retraced his path through the kitchen, along the narrow corridor, and up the rear steps.

It required a number of minutes for the pressman to reach the front of No 11. He had to traverse the alleyway, turn the corner, and walk along the pavement to the house. Observing through a small gap between the red velvet curtains of the sitting-room window, Holmes and I eagerly awaited his appearance.

A wooden mantel clock marked the seconds as we stared through the glass. At last, after what seemed like an eternity, Holmes nudged my arm. There in his flat cap and heavy coat came the American. Displaying a slight limp, he ambled towards the front gate with yet another unlit cigar butt between his lips. He must have had a pocket full of the wretched things!

We continued to watch as Davis tossed the butt into the street and at the foot of the black-asphalt pathway nodded a silent greeting to the constable guarding the door. To our great amazement, the American then drew from his coat pocket a small penknife with an ivory-coloured handle.

The gate and its latch were anchored to a pair of white plaster columns, one of which held the brass plaque containing the house number that we had passed in the fog. It was upon this plaque that, as calm as could be, Davis began operating with his knife. The pilaster blocked our view of his exact movements, but it seemed perfectly obvious that he was doing his best to liberate the plaque from its mounting place.

"Hoy!" bellowed the constable. "You there! What are you up to?"

Davis continued his machinations, seemingly so intent as to not having heard the policeman's shouts.

The constable cried out again: "What are you doing there?"

As if interrupted in some intense endeavour, Davis stopped his work, removed his cap, and slowly addressed the policeman in an unidentifiable conglomeration of English accents. "Beggin' your pardon, guvnor. Everybody's talkin' 'bout the murders in that 'ouse, and there are those wot would pay lots of money for this-'ere address-plate — it being from the murder scene and all." Then he replaced his cap and resumed the plaque's removal.

At the cheek of this vagabond, the constable stomped down the few steps to the asphalt walkway and marched to the gate. Along the way, he muttered expletives loud enough for us to hear through the wooden door.

Once the policeman reached the pilaster under attack, Holmes commanded, "*Now*, Watson!" and the two of us rushed over to the small, wooden post-box. "No time to pick the lock," Holmes murmured, "simple as it is." And with that, he delivered a sharp, high kick that smashed the box into pieces.

Though neither man outside turned his head, I jumped at the decisiveness of Holmes' act. Yet even more of a shock — to Holmes as well as to me — was what we found.

Nothing. The box was empty.

"But Davis told us that he had seen a letter delivered here this morning," I said.

"Clearly," said Holmes, "someone has been here before us. It is the only explanation."

Chapter Six

Developments

Royalty is either royal or it is nothing.
— Richard Harding Davis
Our English Cousins

i

"Come quickly, Watson," whispered Holmes, motioning for me to follow. Back through the kitchen we hurried and then down the narrow corridor leading to the rear door. "We must find the postman," he said once we were outside. "His next delivery should be quite soon."

Upon reaching the end of the alleyway, we turned towards Boston Street. At the corner of the pavement that stretched out before the row of houses, it was easy to spot Davis still engaged with the bewildered policeman in front of No. 11. Yet Holmes pointed beyond the two. "There, Watson. Do you see him?"

I looked up the street and immediately recognised the grey-uniformed representative of Her Majesty's postal service plodding towards us, the heavy, leather mailbag on his right shoulder causing him to list slightly in that direction.

There would be no trouble reaching him before he arrived at No. 11; but in order to sidestep the continuing drama between Davis and the constable, Holmes and I took to the center of the roadway, returning to the pavement just in time to intercept our target—a short, round little man who carried the mailbag proudly.

"Have you the post for No. 11?" Holmes asked him.

"What is it about No. 11?" cried the postman in a high-pitched voice, scarcely slowing his pace. "You're the second bloke today asking me about it. And I will tell you, as I told *him*: I'm not at liberty to discuss the Royal Mail with civilians."

"My name is Sherlock Holmes," replied my friend.

The announcement stopped the postman in his tracks. "Sherlock Holmes, the detective?" he asked, peering up at my friend from under the shiny, black peak of his cap.

"The same."

The postman beamed. "I have indeed heard your name, sir. I follow your adventures in *The Strand*. If I can be of service — without compromising my authority, you understand — I'd be most obliged to help."

"I am investigating the pair of murders that took place in No. 11 on Saturday night," explained Holmes. He believed that giving up a small amount of information generally netted useful details in response.

"A *pair* of murders, you say?" The postman raised his thick eyebrows in appreciation of the enormity of the crimes. He was a short man, but suddenly — in spite of the heavy mailbag weighing him down — he was standing tall in his postal greys. "First I've heard of it. Saturday night, you say?"

Holmes nodded. "The letters from your previous rounds — they are no longer in your possession. Can you tell me if you have already delivered any mail to No. 11 this morning?"

Here the postman took a moment to scrutinise my friend. "No harm there, I suppose," he said at last. "Yes, sir, I did make a delivery there earlier today. It was on my second round some time before noon."

"Was there anything unusual about the post, can you say?"

"Funny you should ask, sir. The stamp — double-eagle it had on it. From Russia. I keep a lookout for unusual stamps. To tell the truth, I'm a bit of a philatelist, you see. Of the amateur variety."

Holmes' steel-grey eyes sparked as they always did when he uncovered a clue. "Did the name of the sender appear on the outside?"

"The sender? No, sorry, sir. Not that I noted."

"What about the postmark?" I put in, trying to anticipate Holmes' next question.

"It would have been printed with Cyrillic letters, Watson," Holmes explained. "Impossible to decipher into English."

The postman shook his head. "I told you I am an amateur philatelist, Mr. Holmes. I may not be able to understand Russian, but I can certainly recognise the names of key Russian cities no matter the peculiarities of the lettering."

Holmes clapped his hands together. Excellent!" he cried. Then with no apparent logic that I could see, he asked, "Do you know if the letter came from Kronstadt?"

"Kronstadt?" The postman shook his head again. "No. I'm certain it was postmarked in St Petersburg."

"'St Petersburg,'" Holmes repeated. Then he said, "Thank you very much indeed. You've been a great help."

The postman readjusted his leather bag. "What about that other bloke — the one who was asking about No. 11? He demanded that I hand over the post. Might he have been the — the murderer?" The deep crease in his brow indicated his degree of concern.

"I wouldn't worry about that," said Holmes. "But you've provided key information, and I thank you very much indeed."

We left the postman behind, his frown of consternation metamorphosing into a look of accomplishment. I was set to ask Holmes about Kronstadt when he pointed down the street. "What do you say, Watson? Don't you think it's time we rescue Mr. Davis from the clutches of the law?"

"Or rather," I countered, "rescue the law from the clutches of Mr. Davis."

By the time we reached the bickering pair, the constable had already got Davis — or rather the ruffian Davis appeared to be — to hand over the penknife. The blade was not very big, but one can appreciate the anxiety the thing must have produced in the policeman. As for the brass plate, though scratched a bit, it remained affixed to the pilaster.

Just as Holmes was about to intervene — I suspected he would try offering his name again, which was especially well known to the police throughout the area near Baker Street — a hansom came to rest in front of us, and out climbed Inspector Lestrade. The constable immediately stood at attention.

"Inspector Lestrade," Holmes said, identifying the policeman for the benefit of Davis.

"I reckoned I'd find you here," Lestrade said to Holmes. "Your page-boy told me as much when I stopped at Baker Street. But who's this then?" he asked, narrowing his eyes to scrutinise the roughly dressed Davis standing off to the side.

The putative villain straightened up and offered a military salute. "Richard Harding Davis, at your service, *sir*."

Lestrade's eyebrows shot up in wonder. "Not the pressman who was with Mr. Holmes at the murder scene Saturday night?"

"Yes, sir. That's me."

I cannot say which policeman was more surprised, the perplexed inspector who had his own view of what reporters should look like or the poor constable who had been so involved in arguing with the now complacent scoundrel.

"I must say," Lestrade observed, "you don't look the part."

"No, sir," said Davis his chin jutting outward. "I'm in mufti — so to speak — in order to help Mr. Holmes with his inquiries."

A few words of explanation from Lestrade calmed the agitated constable, and the Inspector sent him back to guarding the door. Then Lestrade turned to us. "Owens, the missing butler," he announced, "came to the Yard himself not an hour ago, he did. I thought you might be interested in the news, Mr. Holmes."

"Quite so, Lestrade. What did he have to say for himself?"

"Strange, really. Said he felt safer in police custody than in the streets."

"Did he have anything to add about his behaviour Saturday night? Did he tell you why he had run off or who owns this house?"

"No. Never met the owner, he says. Admitted that he'd been too drunk to remember much of anything that night. Though he did say that all his orders come by post from somebody—presumably, the owner—who lives in Russia."

Russia — the origin of the letter which the postman had described. Still, I reasoned, *better to keep such thoughts to myself.* There was no need to inform Lestrade of our talk with the postman. It was just the sort of detail that might wind up revealing to the police our illegal entry into No. 11.

The Marquis of Putnam died later that same Monday evening. On the following morning, doctors deemed young Cyril Ingraham, now the new Marquis, well enough to leave St. Bart's. Unfortunately, he would be returning to Ulster Place not only to recuperate, but also — following the inquest concerning his older brother's death — to arrange the funerals of both his father and his brother.

Like the doctors, the police also allowed the young Earl his freedom. Even though the death of the patriarch underscored the new Marquis' financial motive for removing his older brother from the line of succession, Lestrade concluded that there were no legal grounds for keeping the new Lord Putnam under police watch any longer. Besides, with Owens the butler having presented himself at Scotland Yard, the authorities had another suspect to consider.

It was just such suspicions that prompted Lestrade to arrange a meeting between Holmes and the butler Tuesday afternoon in the turreted, red-brick headquarters of Scotland Yard. A uniformed officer led us to the cramped room Lestrade had reserved for the occasion.

Owens was already seated at a table opposite the Inspector when we entered. The butler was dressed in a dark suit; but out of his formal livery, the grey-haired man looked less authoritative than one expects a butler to appear. He seldom met one's eye and in answering questions seemed woefully uninformed on matters concerning his employer for whose various affairs he was supposedly responsible. Compared to the inebriated state in which we had found him on Saturday night, however, on this occasion he reasonably resembled someone who might actually be charged with overseeing a household.

"I was employed by a gentleman I never met," Owens explained, "a man called Ivan Ivanov who spent much of his time in Russia. An agency directed me to Boston Street, and I received my specific instructions by mail. I was to oversee the house, instruct Cook when elaborate meals were required, and inform my employer by post regarding the comings and goings of Miss Tamarova who lived there."

Holmes cocked an eyebrow. "A bit strange, wouldn't you agree — to report so closely on a woman's activities to an absentee landlord?"

Owens shrugged. "Not for me to say, sir, is it? Mr. Ivanov paid well, and I performed my duties as he required me to do."

"And what did you report?"

"Not much *to* report, was there? Except for the exchange of letters between her and the Earl of Ingraham, that rich fellow who went mountain-climbing in South America."

"But people believed the Earl was dead," I pointed out.

Irritated at the contradiction, Owens folded his arms across his chest. "Beggin' your pardon, sir," he said, his voice turning brittle as he addressed me, "but people don't always know everything, do they? Miss Tamarova was quite open with me. Newspaper accounts to the contrary, she knew that he was alive and coming home; and I communicated this information to Mr. Ivanov."

"Your reports were not made known to her?" Holmes asked.

"No, sir. She never suspected that I was sending this news along to anyone else."

"You were a sort of watchdog, I should say," Lestrade offered.

The butler shrugged.

"To which Russian city were you sending your letters?" Holmes asked.

"St Petersburg."

"As I suspected," Holmes said with a nod. "And it was in search of a letter from St Petersburg that you approached the postman yesterday morning?"

"Why, yes," said the butler, eyebrows raised at the extent of Holmes' knowledge. Quickly, he changed the subject. "By the time that Earl came by Saturday night, I was good and drunk. I don't know what happened after he got there — just that I should get out."

"Smart fellow," muttered Lestrade.

"I've been sharing a flat with a friend of mine in Kentish Town since I left the house that night. Maybe I was followed in the fog. But some time Sunday I received a note. It was slipped under the door. It said a letter from Russia was arriving Monday morning — that is, yesterday — at Boston Street. When I'd picked it up, I should walk back to the flat. Before I got there, I would be stopped by the man who wanted it, and I should give it to him."

"And you followed these instructions?" Lestrade said.

Owens laughed drily. "Oh, yes. At least, I tried. But I never retrieved the letter, you see."

"And when you failed at picking up the post," the policeman said, "you came to us."

"For protection," the butler agreed. "Better than risking my life by walking back to the flat empty-handed."

"Do you still have the note?" asked Holmes.

"No," Owens answered with a sardonic smile. "Burned it, I did. 'Nothing left to incriminate me' is my motto. But I assure you, gentlemen — you can believe it when I say that I memorised the last line: 'You know what happens to people who cross me.' It was signed 'Ivanov'."

Lestrade sighed and stroked his chin.

"And now you lot," Owens added with a snarl, "are holding me for murder."

The policeman grinned in response.

"We're done here, Lestrade," Holmes said grimly as he got to his feet. "Hang on to Owens — for his own good if nothing else."

Lestrade also rose and placed a hand on the butler's shoulder. "He's safe with us, Mr. Holmes."

To me, Holmes said, "I think we should be paying our respects to the mourners at Ulster Terrace. In addition to offering our condolences, I am hoping that the new Marquis may be able to furnish us with more information concerning this mystery man from Russia. On the way, I shall stop to send a message to the Bath Hotel. I would like Mr. Davis to join us as well. It's time for him to see how he is connected to all these goings-on."

Sherlock Holmes and I made our way down a long corridor, through the foyer, and out to Whitehall. Amidst the chaos of late-afternoon traffic, I hailed a hansom, and Holmes informed the driver of our destinations — first, a post office for sending the telegram to Davis and then Ulster Terrace for meeting with the new Marquis of Putnam.

As our cab clattered down the roadway, I pondered what questions Holmes intended to ask His Lordship. Little did I realise that such questions would prove trivial compared with the drama about to unfold once Richard Harding Davis arrived on the scene.

Chapter Seven

The Marquis and the Pressman

In America it is every one for himself. In England it is every one
for everyone else, and though the individual may occasionally
suffer, the majority rejoice.

— Richard Harding Davis
Our English Cousins

i

Richard Harding Davis agreed to meet us in Ulster
Terrace at five o'clock. Arriving a few minutes before the
hour, Holmes and I began pacing to and fro in anticipation
of the pressman's arrival. By then, night had fallen and
wisps of fog were drifting along the street.

Some ten minutes later, a hansom rolled to the kerb;
and Davis, bedecked in Inverness cape, climbed out.

"There he is, Holmes," said I, pointing at the figure
who was just then pausing in the yellow glow of a gas lamp
to confirm the time on his fancy wrist-watch. Strangely, with
his sharply-chiselled profile and standing almost six feet tall
in that traditional dark cape, the man might have been
mistaken for Sherlock Holmes. Davis appeared to be what

the Americans call a "dead-ringer" — especially in the gloom of a cold and foggy winter's eve.

One could not tell if it was the chill in the air or more probably his sciatica that caused Davis to traverse the pavement with a noticeable limp. But whatever the cause, it seemed apparent that on this night his walking stick was bound to serve as more than a mere fashionable accessory. At the time, little could I appreciate the prescience of my observation.

We were about to approach the man when Holmes caught my arm, indicating with a flick of his head a movement in the mist to Davis' right.

I too then noted a break in the fog, and suddenly a shadowy form exploded out of the murk.

A phantom? I remember thinking. *A bogeyman?*

What I actually saw was a long, black coat, a small-brimmed hat, and the glint of a knife blade raised high. Then, before either Holmes or I could even shout a warning, the creature sprang at Davis.

But the pressman was equally quick. The athletic Davis — an American footballer at Lehigh University, I would later learn — parried the attack with his stick. Down came the knife, but Davis subverted the arc of the blow, causing the blade to tear into his left shoulder instead of the centre of his chest.

"Davis!" I shouted as the attacker bolted.

Holmes moved to follow the villain, but the assailant was too fast. Rushing into the fog, he disappeared in the direction of Regent's Park.

"He — he thought I was you," Davis cried out to Holmes as I put my arm round the man to keep him upright. "'Here's for you, Sherlock Holmes,' he hissed in my ear just before he struck.

"Let's get him inside," I said, but Holmes was insistent.

"I must know, Davis. Did you detect an accent? Russian perhaps?"

"No," Davis winced. "Maybe . . . American. Or English. I'm not sure."

"Enough!" I cried. "We have to take him into the house where I can have a look at his wound."

Had Davis' survival instincts not prevailed, the damage would surely have been fatal. As it was, I saw him grasp his shoulder where blood was trickling down between his fingers and onto his cape.

ii

We pounded on the front door and clanged the bell; and thanks to Cyril Ingraham's quick instructions to his servants, I was able to procure what I needed to dress Davis' wound. Fortunately, the knife had hit no vital organs; and once I stripped away his blood-mottled shirt, the small cut required but a few sutures to close and bandage.

Soon I was guiding a pale and shaken Richard Harding Davis into the library where in front of bookshelves that reached to the ceiling stood Sherlock Holmes and the

115

new Marquis of Putnam. Though a few strips of bandaging still appeared on His Lordship's brow, the Marquis looked much stronger than he had in hospital just two days before. Davis, I might add, wore a white shirt that had been provided by His Lordship. It was a trifle small and pulled across his stomach, but Davis — however much the clothes-horse — was not complaining.

"Your Lordship," Holmes said, "may I present to you the American writer, Mr. Richard Harding Davis."

The two men shook hands.

"Glad to see you on your feet, Davis," Lord Putnam said.

"As a rule," replied the American with a forced smile, "I prefer vertical to horizontal." Then he pointed to his shirt. "Thanks for this. Quite the noble gesture — shirt off your back and all that."

His Lordship offered an embarrassed shrug. At the same time, Davis relied on my arm and his walking stick to settle himself in the nearest armchair.

Once we were all seated, I took the lead in offering our sympathies. "Your Lordship, before we discuss the terrible events that have just occurred, we must first express our condolences to you. Though we celebrate the British tradition of exalting the new, we cannot fail to mourn the passing of the old."

A look of pain crossed the face of the young Marquis. "I appreciate your sentiments, gentlemen. Though my father had been ill for quite a while, the end, whilst not unexpected, still comes as a shock." He paused to catch his breath, then changed the subject. "We must now turn our attention to the living and the attack on Mr. Davis."

"True enough," said Holmes, turning to face the American. "Our sympathies go out to you, Mr. Davis, yet it should not be forgotten that, as you yourself have revealed, the assault in question was aimed at *me*. Since the Boston Street murders constitute my only case for the moment, one can reasonably infer that our investigations have brought us closer to the murderer than he would like us to be."

"But who can be behind all these acts, Mr. Holmes?" His Lordship asked. "My brother and Miss Tamarova murdered; Mr. Davis — in your stead — almost so."

"I had a plan in mind before this most recent attack," said Holmes. "The assault upon Mr. Davis merely makes it all the more urgent. I suggest we go back to where this case actually started — literally."

"Ah," Davis sighed, an exhalation born from recognition or from pain — I could not tell which. "King's Cross Railroad Station. Where I left for the ill-fated trip to Lincolnshire. The platform —"

"No," said Holmes, shaking his head. "Before that — where you *first* heard of this business regarding the necklace."

"Do you mean the High Table?"

"Precisely," said Holmes. "Tomorrow is Wednesday. I shall ask my brother to arrange admission tomorrow evening for Dr. Watson and myself at the High Table Club. Mycroft will know those in charge who can fulfil my requests. On this occasion, he shall ask the Club to break with tradition and allow entry to some personages not on the membership list. You, Mr. Davis, are already an honorary member and will have no problem — as long as you feel strong enough to attend."

Davis laughed, wincing again. "Never fear. I want to know who did this to me. I'll be there."

Holmes turned to His Lordship. "I trust, My Lord, that you too will be able to join us."

"I will indeed!" exclaimed Cyril Ingraham, banging his fist on the arm of his chair for emphasis. "I must learn who killed my brother. However much it may look to the contrary, I never wanted to be the Marquis of Putnam. The title rightfully belongs — belonged — to Chet, and I will never rest till I find the blackguard who killed him. I am convinced that my father would have wanted the same."

Holmes turned again to the American. "To recreate the beginning as accurately as possible, Mr. Davis, you must see to it that your friend, Lieutenant Stanton, is also in attendance."

"Of course, Mr. Holmes. I'll do my best. But he may have already begun his return to Russia, you see, and not be available."

"Oh," said Holmes, "I wouldn't trouble myself on that account. I believe you will find him not only very much still in London, but also with a calendar that is free tomorrow evening."

Davis looked quizzically at Sherlock Holmes. I knew my friend well enough to recognise that he must have already communicated these plans to his brother — probably when he had gone to see Mycroft Sunday evening to return the Queen's necklace. Owing to Mycroft's political connections, it would have been child's play for him to arrange with the American Embassy to have Stanton at the ready Wednesday night for whatever instructions might come his way, directly or indirectly, from either one of the Holmes brothers or even from Richard Harding Davis if it were so required.

Holmes nodded at Lord Putnam who rose, and then so did the rest of us. "Tomorrow evening then, gentlemen," said Holmes.

Davis had relied upon his stick to stand, and I escorted him to the outer door. A footman provided Holmes and me with our coats and Davis his bloodied cape. Once more expressing our sympathies to the new Marquis, we exited into the chill night.

A thin rain was falling, but it did not prevent any of us from noting the man approaching on the flags. At first, my guard was up. The attack on Davis had not been too long before. But then I noted that neither the Trilby nor the turned-up collar could hide the curls of the moustache.

"He's the fellow from the High Table," Davis whispered, "the one with the black-pearl stud."

Clearly, Sir Roderick Childs could not go undetected, and we nodded brief salutations as we passed.

"Condolences, don't you know," Sir Roderick said.

"He seems to be everywhere we are," I muttered once we were out of earshot.

"*Almost* everywhere," Holmes corrected and moved towards the kerb.

The fancy carriage and pair of black horses awaiting us put Sir Roderick out of mind. Given the injured Davis and the continuing rain, we were most fortunate indeed that the Marquis had offered us such elegant transportation. To be sure, Baker Street was close by, but Holmes directed the driver to Piccadilly and Arlington Street first, so he and I could be certain of our injured comrade's safe arrival at the Bath Hotel.

Davis tried to dismiss me once he exited the carriage. But after insisting on helping him reach the lobby, I left him only after one of the porters offered him an arm. It seemed reasonable to assume that between the porter's support and Davis' walking stick, the American could successfully negotiate the journey to his rooms.

Pluck and mettle, indeed.

Chapter Eight

The High Table Club

[Detective Ford's] position was similar
to that of the dramatic critic. The dramatic critic
warned the public against bad plays;
Ford warned it against bad men.
-Richard Harding Davis
"The Amateur"

i

Wednesday afternoon.

To direct my thoughts away from the drama scheduled for later that evening, I tried to keep myself occupied. Under threatening black clouds in the morning, I visited my surgery; and braving a light rain in the afternoon, I consumed extra time by walking back to Baker Street beneath my umbrella rather than hiring a cab. What is more, I took the opportunity to stop at Bradley's in Oxford Street to refill my supply of Arcadia mixture.

Yet neither my own diversions nor the scratchings from Holmes' violin could prevent me from pondering the questions that had filled my head since waking that morning, questions that I hoped would be answered later that evening at the High Table: *Would Sherlock Holmes identify the murderer of the late Rochester Ingraham and Natasha Tamarova? Would someone among the invited confess? Would we discover the identity of the Russian who owned the house in Boston Street or, for that matter, the unknown person who had rushed past us in the fog as we approached the entrance to No. 11? Why had the mysterious Sir Roderick Childs appeared so frequently? Had he been dogging our tracks? And what of the villain who had attacked Richard Harding Davis whilst mistaking him for Holmes?*

I for one had no clue regarding the answers. The murky London Particular in which this entire business began seemed quite the fitting metaphor to describe the thick haze in which I currently found myself.

ii

Appropriately enough, it was no longer rain that filled the streets when Holmes and I drove to the High Table that evening. Rather, random tendrils of fog coiled about our boots as we exited the hansom in Pall Mall just past Waterloo Place.

In point of fact, we were but a matter of yards from Mycroft's original club, the Diogenes, which was located closer to St James's Street at the western end of the road. Given the desire for solitude among the Diogenes' members,

I have always tempered my descriptions of the club's façade — however unassuming it is in reality — to prevent the curious from discovering its precise location. Oh, the pilgrim seeking to identify the establishment may look for a bow window somewhere between St James's Street and the Carlton Club, but such a detail is in reality a minor clue.[7]

The approach to the High Table offers even less to describe. With anonymity paramount to its distinguished members, the club's only access is a lacklustre oaken door somewhat east of the Carlton. Painted black when we approached it, the door appeared nondescript in an otherwise ordinary grey plastered wall. Whilst other clubs posted liveried doormen beneath arched porticos, no such sentinel or structure appeared before the High Table.

(I can attest first-hand that in December of '97 a knock on the oaken door by the *cognoscenti* would summon a sombre figure in black to offer admittance. Unfortunately, having never returned to the place since that memorable evening, I am unable to present any clues concerning its current admission procedures.)

Following our knock, Holmes and I were immediately granted entry; yet we were stopped just inside the door by a portly major-domo whose grey side-whiskers covered most of his cheeks and whose thick spectacles

---

[7] For more information on the precise whereabouts of the Diogenes Club, see David Marcum's "Pall Mall: Specifically Locating the Diogenes Club," in *The Baker Street Journal*, Vol. 67, No. 2, Summer 2017. (DDV)

clouded his eyes. It appeared to be his job to check our names against a pre-arranged list.

Scrutinising us from crown to toe, he clucked twice as he marked ticks next to our names on the short list he held close before him. Then with a nod, he gestured for us to follow. Obviously, Mycroft had pulled the proper strings — no one to be admitted this night without prior approval.

As Davis had previously described, a short corridor took us past a small smoking room replete with crystal ashtrays and leather-cushioned chairs. Yet, surprisingly, in light of our own specific business in the club that evening, the chamber was not empty.

Perhaps "surprisingly" is not the appropriate word, for it was rather unsurprising indeed that occupying one of the deep leather armchairs was the very man who seemed to have been trailing after us throughout much of our investigation. From above the curled dark moustache of Sir Roderick Childs, two piercing eyes looked up from the book he was reading.

Holmes cocked an eyebrow, eliciting a defensive response from our guide.

"Sir Roderick Childs," the major-domo whispered. "A Baronet and Member of Parliament."

"I know who he is," Holmes shot back loudly. "In fact, I half-expected him to be here. But how did he get in? The uninvited were not to be admitted tonight."

"Very sorry, indeed, Mr. Holmes," said the *maître d'*, his glasses reflecting the gas lamps within the smoking room, "but Sir Roderick was not, as you said, 'admitted tonight'. He's been in attendance all day and has refused to leave. It is the Baronet's custom to spend his free time with us until he is summoned to Westminster for a vote. The

Conservative Party know they can find him here; and when he is needed, they fetch him back to Parliament. Later tonight, you see, a major vote is expected."

Without looking up, Sir Roderick intoned, "The Navy Increase Bill. I support it and expect a hansom to be sent round later to transport me to the House. When it arrives, I shall be out of your hair." He immediately grew silent and resumed his reading.

"Crime novels are his passion," added the major-domo,

Overhearing these words as well, the Baronet held up the volume. "Must find out what happens, don't you know."

Strange though his presence may have been, I beamed upon observing the title on the spine. It was my very own *The Sign of Four.*

"I'd give a thousand pounds," the man murmured loud enough for me to hear, "no, five thousand pounds, for another mystery like this one."

What higher praise can I receive? I asked myself—and from a Member of Parliament no less.

Sherlock Holmes, on the other hand, was not pleased. "See that Sir Roderick stays out of our affairs," he told our guide brusquely.

The major domo nodded, and without further comment we followed him into the darkened interior of the dining room.

iii

The gas-lit sconces mounted every few feet on the dark wall-panels did little to illuminate the scene; nor did the flickering candles on the otherwise long and bare dark-wood communal table. Even so, there was enough light to reveal the sombre figures seated in the bow-back chairs behind it.

The club's dictum requiring those at the communal table to speak to one another was clearly being ignored. Each personage sat silently, looking up only to inspect us newcomers: At one end, as handsome as ever in formal dinner dress, Richard Harding Davis — the epitome of the Gibson Man (even with his arm in a sling); at the other end, the new Marquis of Putnam, in less formal tweed and still displaying a small white dressing upon his forehead.

Positioned next to Davis was a stranger to me, a handsome young man of military bearing. He was attired in navy-blue, his coat-front marked by two vertical columns of gilt buttons, the coat's collar encircling his neck. A gold aiguillette hung on his left side. With American military patches on the upper arms at each shoulder, this man was obviously Davis' friend, the naval *aide-de-camp*, Lieutenant Robert Stanton. To my surprise, Owens, the butler from Boston Street, was also in attendance as was a vaguely familiar bald-headed man in a well-worn blue-serge suit.

I took the empty seat next to the Marquis, but Holmes remained standing to address the entire group. "Gentlemen," he began, glancing at each man in turn, "thank you for attending." He then proceeded to introduce each person at the table.

I had identified everyone there except for the balding fellow — a man called Higgins — whom Holmes now presented as the postman who delivered the mail in Boston Street, the amateur collector of postage stamps. Without his grey cap and uniform, I simply failed to recognise him though we had met the previous day.

"Let us get to the bottom of this nasty business as quickly as we can, shall we?" Holmes said. "Tonight we will learn who murdered the Earl of Ingraham — that is, the older brother of the new Marquis of Putnam — and the woman with whom the late Earl had once been involved — crimes that one way or another touch each of you."

Suddenly, a flurry of whispers sprang up outside the doorway. With furrows of annoyance creasing his brow, Holmes turned to stare at the commotion. The *maître d',* it appeared, was engaged in a spirited but hushed conversation with the man we had just left in the smoking room.

"Sir Roderick," Holmes intervened, "with the number of times you have involved yourself in the business we are discussing here tonight, you too should have a seat at the table."

The *maître d'* turned away in frustration; but the ubiquitous Sir Roderick Childs, employing my book to give his dramatic moustache a self-conscious pat, slowly entered the room. "Only for a minute or two," he announced defensively. "I shall have to leave for a vote in Parliament. The Navy Increase Bill is due up at any moment."

The Baronet took the empty chair next to Higgins, which the postman pulled out so Sir Roderick could be seated. Everyone else at the table looked at the newcomer.

"Gentlemen," said Holmes by way of explanation, "we add to the mix Sir Roderick Childs —to say the least, an interested spectator."

No one uttered a word of welcome. Davis and Stanton, in fact, eyed the man suspiciously, Davis already having remembered him from the Baronet's presence when the Queen's necklace had first been discussed. I myself began to wonder if Holmes had not presumed the man would be there from the start.

For now, however, the distraction had been settled, and Holmes resumed his presentation. "My Lord," said he to the young Marquis, "please be so kind as to explain to all concerned what business your brother had with the woman in question. Watson and I have heard the story before, but the rest of the gentlemen here deserve to know."

The new Lord Putnam cleared his throat. "I met with my brother at his hotel in the late afternoon on the day of the murders. It was then that he told me about a disturbing letter he had received months before — whilst he was off climbing mountains in Ecuador. The letter came from Natasha Tamarova, a woman with whom he had once been in love. She had discovered how to reach him through the Alpine Club and implored him to come back to her. She was gravely ill, she told him, and only the pleasure of his company could restore her to health."

"A familiar romantic lure," Robert Stanton observed with a cocked eyebrow. Sir Roderick nodded sympathetically as Stanton added, "I'm surprised he fell for it."

Lord Putnam turned to face the lieutenant. "A tired ruse to be certain, sir, but effective nonetheless. And yet even after learning what he believed to be such distressing news, my brother made no effort to hurry back to England. It took months for him to finally write to the woman that he was arriving in London on 17th December — Friday last, that is — and that he would be visiting her the following day."

Stanton slowly shook his head as listened to the plot unfold.

"When my brother and I spoke Saturday evening," Lord Putnam continued, "he assured me that as soon as I left, he was planning to see Miss Tamarova in order to end matters between them once for all. It was during his meeting with her that both of them were killed . . . ."

His Lordship's voice trailed off, and Holmes took advantage of the silence to confront the butler. "Owens, inform everyone here what role you played in this tragedy."

The butler's eyes popped wide. "I had naught to do with any such thing. All I did was to follow my instructions."

"And what instructions were those?"

"As I told you before, it was the employment agency that issued the initial orders. I was to assemble what staff I needed to look after the house and do whatever my employer required."

"And just what was it that this employer required?"

"He left me written orders along with a postal address in Russia. I was to keep him informed of Miss Tamarova's comings and goings. When she told me at the start of this month that the Earl of Ingraham was returning to England on the 17th, I wrote him with the news."

"*Him*?" the Marquis shouted. "Who is this *'him'*? You speak in riddles, man!"

Albeit more calmly, Holmes repeated the question, "Who is this man you were writing to?"

With a slow shake of his head, Owens seemed to shrink in his chair. "Beggin' your pardon, My Lord," said the butler softly to the Marquis, "but as I've said right along, I never set eyes on him. I—I was told by the agency that my employer was a Russian gentleman called Ivan Ivanov."

"*Ivan Ivanov*," Sir Roderick laughed as he sat twiddling the black-pearl stud in his shirt-front. "As common a name in Russia as John Smith is here in England."

"I'm sure I wouldn't know, sir," Owens replied with a shrug. "All I was told was that Mr. Ivanov lived in St. Petersburg and was responsible for the welfare of the young woman, Miss Tamarova, who was staying in the house."

"And to what specific address in St Petersburg," asked Holmes, "did you send the information about Miss Tamarova?"

"To a post office."

Where all this was leading I could not guess. Neither could the two Americans in the room, for they were whispering back and forth and shaking their heads. Finally, Lieutenant Stanton spoke up.

"Mr. Holmes, I don't see the need for my presence here. I only came by in the first place to help out my friend, Mr. Harding Davis. But I have pressing matters to attend to for my government. The mystery man in question is a Russian gentleman; and if my accent doesn't prove my nationality, then surely my uniform will convince you that I am no Russian."

"A few minutes more," Holmes requested and turned to the postman. "Mr. Higgins, you delivered the post to No. 11 in Boston Street on the morning of 20th December — that is, Monday of this week. In other words, two days ago."

Sir Roderick leaned back to get a better view of the man sitting next to him.

"Right you are, Mr. Holmes," Higgins answered. "I do four rounds every morning. On the third, I carried a single envelope to No. 11."

"Tell everyone here, Mr. Higgins, the nature of the stamp, just as you told Dr. Watson and me Monday morning."

Higgins smiled at the simplicity of the task. "It was a *Russian* stamp, Mr. Holmes," he said proudly. "And because I can recognise some of their funny letters, I could tell it was postmarked in St Petersburg."

Holmes now addressed the naval officer Stanton. "I have been told, sir, that your office is in Kronstadt —near the Russian naval base there. Is that correct?"

The American surveyed the faces at the table before answering. "Yes, Mr. Holmes. Kronstadt naval base is an ideal location for business between the Russian and American fleets to take place."

"Kronstadt is on an island, is that not so?"

"Indeed, Kotlin Island."

"But you do not live on this island."

As Stanton answered what was in reality a statement, he once more surveyed the faces. "No, I don't live on the island."

"In what city is it that you actually do live?" asked Holmes.

To students of geography, the answer was eminently predictable. In point of fact, it was Sir Roderick who answered. "St. Petersburg. The two are adjacent."

"Quite so," offered Holmes.

Mr. Higgins and the butler raised their eyebrows.

"That is correct," Stanton agreed.

"And how long," Holmes persisted, "does it generally take you to reach Kronstadt?"

"A few hours by carriage and boat — longer in the snow — though you must understand that I make the trip just a few times a month."

The actual number of occasions Stanton travelled to Kronstadt did not interest Holmes. In fact, Holmes was already asking about another trip the American was used to making. "And how long," Holmes wanted to know, "is required for you to reach London by railway from St Petersburg?"

I was well aware that Holmes already knew the answer. He had made the journey himself years earlier to see his friend, the detective Porfiry Petrovitch, in connection with a pair of gruesome axe-murders.[8]

---

[8] See Dr. Watson's narrative, *Sherlock Holmes and the Shadows of St Petersburg*. (DDV)

"About three days," came the reply.

"Can't be done much faster," Sir Roderick agreed, tapping the cover of my book for emphasis.

To the suspicious mind, the Baronet seemed to know a lot about the peripheries of the case.

At the same time, Richard Harding Davis turned to face Lieutenant Stanton. Lord Putnam too was now staring at the man.

"Three days," Holmes repeated. "Hardly an impediment, I should think, to maintaining a friendship here in London whilst working in St Petersburg."

"I wouldn't know," Sir Roderick said, slowly shaking his head. "It *is* a great distance."

But the Marquis of Putnam ignored Sir Roderick. Instead, as the import of Holmes' words dawned on him, he trained his eyes on Robert Stanton.

At the same time, Sherlock Holmes pointed a long forefinger at the *aide-de-camp*. "I suggest to you, Lieutenant Stanton, that it was *you*, in addition to Rochester Ingraham — then the primary heir to the Marquis of Putnam — who was infatuated with the unfortunate Miss Tamarova; that it was *you* who secured the house on Boston Street for her to live in, that it was *you* with your government connections who did away with the ownership papers at the Public Record Office so you could not be traced; and to watch over her, it was also *you* who hired Owens here to serve as her butler and to simultaneously spy on her as your secret agent."

To give Stanton his due, he took in all of Holmes' charges without any show of reaction.

"Being inordinately jealous," Holmes continued, "you knew of her relationship with His Lordship's older brother; and when, as instructed, the butler advised you of the late Earl's visit to take place on Saturday the 18th December, you wrote an ill-advised letter to Miss Tamarova informing her of your intention to come to London and deal with your romantic rival.

"You left St Petersburg at the start of last week in order to have plenty of time to confront him. As it so happened, you arrived early enough to have been involved in that meeting in this very room with Mr. Davis and my brother concerning some unrelated business involving a necklace.

"Unfortunately for you, your railway journey got you here well before your letter did; and following the tragic events of Saturday night, you realised the incriminating evidence the letter provided and how it might possibly end up in the hands of the police. First, you commanded Owens to retrieve the letter from the postman early Monday morning. When that plan failed, you yourself returned to Boston Street in hopes of intercepting the post before the police got to it — before *I* got to it, actually."

Lord Putnam rose from his seat. He looked from Holmes to Stanton and back to Holmes. "What does all this mean, Mr. Holmes?"

"I am afraid, Your Lordship," said Sherlock Holmes, once more pointing his finger at the naval officer, "it means that Robert Stanton is the mysterious Ivan Ivanov. More to the point, it means that Robert Stanton is the villain who murdered your brother and Miss Tamarova in the house in Boston Street."

Lord Putnam clenched his fists. "Why, of all the vile, underhanded — " he spat out. Then with nostrils flaring and eyes riveted on Stanton, he stormed towards the man like a lion on the hunt. If His Lordship could have breathed fire, I am certain he would have.

Sir Roderick shot out an ineffectual arm to try to stop the Marquis; but it required a deft roll of the wrist by Richard Harding Davis to pin the point of his stick against Lord Cyril's chest and bring the enraged Marquis to a halt.

That was when I leapt up. Davis' quick action allowed me the chance to secure an arm round Lord Putnam's shoulder and guide him back to his chair. Breathing heavily, the Earl glowered at Stanton.

For his part, Robert Stanton continued to sit motionlessly.

"I'm sorry, Your Lordship," said Holmes with a sardonic smile, "but your display of emotion did not give me the opportunity to complete my accusations — to say how it was also Robert Stanton who, upon mistaking you for your brother at Walsingham House, ran you down with his carriage. Only then did he go to Boston Street to settle his score with Miss Tamarova.

"When he found your brother there as well, the plan became simple. He cut your brother's throat; stabbed the poor Russian woman with a single, well-placed knife thrust; and then made his escape into the fog by pushing his way past Watson, Davis and me just outside the house.

Lord Putnam breathed deeply as he took in Holmes report.

"What is more, Your Lordship," Holmes went on, "judging from the sound of the secretive footsteps I heard at St. Bart's when we visited you there the day after the murders, I believe that Stanton came to the hospital intending to kill you, but was put off by the policeman set up outside your ward."

A loud shriek punctuated this final charge, the protest from Stanton's bow-back chair being shoved backward on the hardwood floor as the American sprang to his feet and rushed to the exit.

I remember thinking at the time how strange it was that in the midst of this dramatic moment the portly *maître d'* chose to fill the doorway — to fill it completely, I should add. Stanton tried pushing past the big man; but there was no getting round his bulk. The *maître d'* could not be moved.

Suddenly, a small knife appeared in Stanton's right hand. It looked to be of similar size to the one that had already cut into Davis. And yet still the *maître d'* would not yield. In spite of his bulk, he deftly grabbed Stanton's right forearm and twisted it behind the Lieutenant's back, twisted it so hard, in fact, that the clang of the blade's hitting the floor was clearly audible.

Only after Inspector Lestrade appeared from behind the large man and placed a firm grip on Stanton's shoulder did the *maître d'* step aside. At the same time, he peeled away his grey whiskers and removed the thick-lensed spectacles.

It seems fitting to give Sir Roderick the final word on the evening's dramatics. In spite of my own suspicions, he was, as his excellent choice in reading should have convinced me, a student of crime writings. Combine such an interest with his *penchant* for being a Nosy Parker — the vote in Parliament he had used as an excuse for staying at the High Table had, in fact, been taken much earlier in the day — and one can understand why he had inserted himself in so much of the investigation.

In the end it was Sir Roderick who trailed after the fleeing American and thus the first in the club to see the *maître d's* clean-shaven, glasses-free face. "I say," Sir Roderick asked, "is that really you, Mycroft?"

That was when I too discerned the true identity of the man who had been guarding the door. It was indeed my friend's older brother.

Chapter Nine

Dénouement

Ev'ry little tot at night,
Is afraid of the dark you know.
Some big Yama man they see,
When off to bed they go.
— Collin Davis
"The Yama Yama Man"
Sung by Bessie McCoy
(1908)

i

"To 1898," said Richard Harding Davis seated before our fire. The sherry came from the bottle of Harveys Bristol Cream, which he had brought to Baker Street for the purpose of welcoming in the New Year.

It had been four days since the year had begun; and though I could report that Lady Brownlow did in fact receive the diamond necklace from the Queen in time for Christmas, I could only wonder what Davis had been doing since mid-December when we had last seen him at the High Table.

I had no worries about his finding opportunities to celebrate. Murders and diamond-thefts notwithstanding, the handsome features, sartorial splendour, and ebony walking stick of the Gibson Man enabled him to cut quite the dashing figure. Moreover, with friends in the theatre like Ethel Barrymore and Cissy Loftus, the convivial bachelor could well be expected to have made merry at Christmas and to have rung in the New Year with vigour. One need have no worries concerning the social life of Richard Harding Davis.

As an author, however, my true concern was with his writing. Though it was really none of my business, I nevertheless dared to ask, "How's your work coming along?"

Davis recognised my anxiety. "Not to worry, Doctor," he cautioned me. "In spite of the recent holidays, I've still managed to maintain my schedule. My new book, *Captain Macklin,* is progressing. Like *Soldiers of Fortune*, it's about Americans fighting in Central America. But I'm taking a different approach in this one. The story begins with my hero getting expelled from the West Point military academy. It's going to be a character study as well a tale of adventure."

"It sounds promising," said I, raising my glass. "Here's to future literary successes."

Davis, however, failed to join me in the toast. "I did come here to celebrate the future, Doctor," said he, slowly putting down his glass and then turning to face Holmes, "but to be honest, I still have some concerns regarding the recent business in Boston Street."

Holmes and I lowered our glasses as well, and my friend nodded for Davis to proceed.

"I don't understand how the theft of the necklace fits into Stanton's story."

"That's because it doesn't," said Holmes. "In the end, the stolen necklace was a mere sideshow. Stanton must have mentioned to his Russian paramour what he had learned about the diamonds at your meeting with him and Mycroft.

"Never one to turn her back on opportunity, Miss Tamarova set out to acquire it on her own. She knew where you were staying, and it could not have been too difficult for her to keep watch until you set off for King's Cross and your subsequent journey north. A yellow mac with green stripes like yours — " here Holmes nodded at the coat in question hanging on a peg near our door — "is not the most difficult mark to follow."

"Come now, Mr. Holmes," Davis said, his face turning red. "I didn't wear so flashy a coat to the train station. From the success of my previous disguise, you ought to know that I do have some common sense. After all, I was on a mission for your Queen."

"To the Queen," I took the opportunity to announce, and this time we all managed to complete the toast with a drink.

Suddenly, Davis put down his glass. "With a yellow mac or without one, gentlemen," he proclaimed, glaring at us all the while, "I am still a reporter. I live to write. And this story of the two murders is one that I feel must be shared with the world."

Holmes cocked a disapproving eyebrow.

"Don't worry, Mr. Holmes. I've done this sort of thing before — turn my real-life experiences into fictions. *Soldiers of Fortune* is simply the most recent example. It's based on what I observed during my trip to Cuba in '86, especially what I learned about the Juragua Iron Company near Santiago. And if sales are any proof, I think you'll agree that I did a pretty fair job."

"Mr. Davis," said Holmes, "no one is disputing your success. But should you write about the murders in Boston Street, I must insist that you maintain the utmost discretion. Delicate relations among Russia, America, and Great Britain hang in the balance. Obviously, I have no objection to your informing the world that Sir Roderick's Navy Increase Bill passed. That's public information."

Davis nodded as he took in Holmes' caveats.

"I think you'll also agree," Holmes continued, "that the private peccadillos within the House of Putnam need no airings, and you really must keep my brother's international connections from the public eye. Nor, for that matter, can there be any links to the British government related to this matter."

Davis studied the drink he was holding as he listened to Holmes.

"In addition," my friend cautioned, "under no circumstances may you refer to the High Table Club by its rightful name."

Davis shook his head. "You're not leaving me with much, are you?" he chuckled. "You do realise that in

America you'd be accused of tampering with our First Amendment."

"Quite so," Holmes replied without even the briefest of smiles.

"Nonetheless," Davis said, palms up to signal compliance, "you may rest assured that I would never dream of breaking a trust with the man who rescued me from a most delicate situation. It's not the way I was brought up. You have my word."

Holmes nodded appreciatively.

"And you also cannot forget your new novel," I felt compelled to add.

"Yes," he said, eyes brightening at the thought. "But even though I believe I'm making progress with it, I got stuck in another pea-souper on Christmas Day, and it reminded me how much I am obsessed by those murders that we discovered in the fog."

Though "pea-soup" remains a tired metaphor, one that I personally have always shunned, I well understood Davis' predicament. "I know exactly what you mean," I told him. "I too wrestle with the dilemma. How often I believe that the entire world yearns to hear the details concerning some intricate criminal investigation — like these Boston Street murders — that I am not at liberty to reveal."

"Your remedy?"

"Disguise and subterfuge. They have become the tools upon which I rely."

"Touché," said Davis.

Thereafter, the three of us drank our sherry in silent contemplation. When the glasses were empty, Davis rose to take his leave. With a cryptic nod, he bade us good evening, donned his yellow mac, and exited our sitting room.

ii

One morning some five weeks later, Billy brought us two important communications. The first appeared in *The Daily Telegraph*.

Holmes and I were having breakfast at the time, and my friend was just clipping off the top of an egg as I opened the newspaper. "I say, Holmes," I announced upon noting the main story, "have you heard the news?"

"The paper's only just got here, old fellow," he replied, selecting a slice of toast from the upright holder. "Still, I am more than certain that you will keep me abreast of the day's important events."

I read to him the following headline: *"Crisis in Cuba: American Battleship Blown up in Havana Harbour."*

"Do tell," said he. "What are the details?"

I continued to read: *"The U.S.S. Maine, an American battle ship, was crippled by explosives in the harbour of Havana some time during the night of 15 February. Over two hundred men are thought to be dead."*

"Two hundred!" lamented Holmes with the shake of his head. "The Spanish are in for it now. The Americans will never allow such effrontery to pass."

No sooner had Holmes made this pronouncement than Billy arrived with the second of the two communications to which I referred. It was a telegram from the Bath Hotel.

I unfolded the yellow paper as soon as the boy had left. "It's from Richard Harding Davis," I announced and read the short text aloud: *"Returning to New York. Then to Cuba to report on the war."*

"Real battles," I said. "It's what he's been craving for years."

As we learned from his reports in the prints, Richard Harding Davis did not actually arrive in Cuba until April. But when he finally did reach the island, his accounts of the conflicts, in some of which — as I have already mentioned — he himself (in spite of his sciatica) actually participated, earned great distinction.

One cannot soon forget Davis' stirring account of Theodore Roosevelt's charge up San Juan Hill in early July. Roosevelt was, according to Davis, the "most conspicuous figure" in the battle. Indeed, not a few distinguished historians have gone so far as to suggest that Roosevelt's ultimate ascendance to the American presidency was due in no small part to Davis' depiction of the heroic colonel in Cuba "mounted high on horseback . . . and quite alone."[9]

---

[9] While in Cuba, Davis encountered Stephen Crane, who was also covering the war. Though unknown to Davis, the American author of *The Red Badge of Courage* was the target of a blackmail campaign that Sherlock Holmes helped resolve. Ironically, Davis did not get on with his fellow writer although he lauded Crane's

Though the Spanish-American War ended not long thereafter, Davis' war correspondence did not. Within two years he was in South Africa reporting on the Second Boer War. In point of fact, he stirred up quite the controversy when in Pretoria he announced his sympathy for the Boers over the British.

"Rather insulting," I said to Holmes. "I should imagine that such a point of view will cost him dearly here in England."

"With all the trouble the man is fostering," Holmes said wistfully, "perhaps he will forget about writing an account of the Boston Street murders."

Though for decades I myself honoured Holmes' request not to publish the story, it was clear that in spite of the political storm Davis had created in South Africa, the journalist had forgotten neither the murders themselves nor our harrowing trek to Boston Street that infamous night through the smothering fog. Somewhere in his consciousness, he had kept these events solidly rooted.

How else to explain that in 1901, four years after the murders, Davis finally did commit to paper his recollections of that fatal night — a story, which appropriately enough he titled "In the Fog"? To be fair to the man, however, just as

---

artistic ability. Davis blamed much of the author's troubles on Crane's common-law wife, Cora, but after Crane's death, Davis praised her love for the man. To read more of Holmes and Watson's involvement with the Cranes and the blackmailing incident, see Watson's *Sherlock Holmes and the Baron of Brede Place*. (DDV)

he had promised, he rendered scarcely recognisable the true nature of the investigation.

Oh, the kernels of the plot remained: the stolen necklace, the double murders, the Russian connection (not to mention two actual references to Sherlock Holmes himself). But in addition to disguising key elements of the case and employing a number of false names to add to the confusion, Davis also managed to add a degree of lightness to the terrible crimes. I will be the first to admit that, thanks to the man's ability to submerge fact in fiction — "reconstituted journalism" one literary critic termed it — his story held my attention from first to last.

Holmes and I never saw Richard Harding Davis again. As I had feared, siding with the Boers had not only caused his honorary memberships at clubs like the Garrick and the High Table to be rescinded, but also alienated many of his British acquaintances. He did return to England upon more than one occasion, yet he maintained an understandable distance from many of his friends and associates, Holmes and me included.

Still, owing to the availability of various American periodicals, we were able to mark from afar the major events in Davis' life. There was his marriage to Cecil Clark, an aspiring artist — as well as their subsequent divorce. There was also his marriage to Bessie McCoy, a vaudeville singer whose sobriquet, the "Yama Yama Girl", reminded me of the attractive music-hall star with whom I had once seen him. ("On the whole," Davis had written in *Our English Cousins* some twenty years before he plucked Bessie off the vaudeville stage, "I consider the music-hall a much misunderstood and undervalued entertainment.") And then there was the birth of Hope, their aptly named daughter.

It seemed that nothing could slow the man down. His journalistic commitment took him to Japan for the Russo-Japanese War and to Vera Cruz for possible hostilities between the United States and Mexico. In 1914 he travelled to Europe to report the early events of the Great War — in particular, the Germans' dastardly invasion of Belgium. "Like a river of steel," he wrote, the German army "cut Brussels in two."

What is more, through it all, the man remained true to his singular self. Within the limited safety of his battlefield tent, he would dine in evening dress and bathe in his portable rubber bathtub. And when searching for stories of combat to report, he would risk being mistaken for a soldier or spy by wearing his military-style suits complete with *faux* medals and high-top boots.

In the end, however, not even such comforting eccentricities could minimise the toll his reportorial adventures took on his sense of honour and fair play. Disillusioned and exhausted by what he had witnessed in Europe, Davis returned to the States in January of 1916. He died in April of that year one week short of his fifty-second birthday.

In Holmes' cottage in Sussex, he and I commemorated the news of the writer's death.

"Let us give Davis the last word," I suggested as my friend poured us each a glass of port. "He has written that the fool and the philosopher are equal." I lifted my glass. "To the fool and the philosopher."

I was about to drink when Holmes interceded. "It's been a few years now, old fellow, and I'm rather afraid that you have forgotten the second part of Davis' pronouncement. The fool and the philosopher are indeed equal," Holmes reminded me as he raised his glass, "but only—as Davis so succinctly put it — at a game of dice."

I contemplated the tawny liquid, and a reluctant laugh escaped my lips.

THE END

The Editor's Suggested Reading

Full appreciation of Dr. Watson's account of the murders in Boston Street must begin with a reading of "In the Fog," Richard Harding Davis' account of the killings — however fictional his treatment of the details. Interested readers may find it on-line at: https://www.gutenberg.org/files/7884/7884-h/7884-h.htm

Arthur Lubow's highly readable biography, *The Reporter Who Would be King,* includes Davis' personal recollection of the foggy evening in question. It must be pointed out, however, that like Davis' fictional narrative, Lubow's reporting does not conform to Watson's account.

For additional analysis of not only Davis' relationship to the London fog but also that of Watson's literary agent, Arthur Conan Doyle, see Christine L. Corton's cleverly titled *London Fog: The Biography, pp. 222-232.*

Finally, for Davis' narrative concerning the world events in the year prior to his meeting Holmes and Watson, see his memoir, *A Year From a Reporter's Note-Book.*

Also from Daniel D Victor

The first four books in the American Literati series:

The Final Page of Baker Street

Sherlock Holmes and The Baron of Brede Place

Seventeen Minutes to Baker Street

The Outrage at The Diogenes Club

Also from Daniel D Victor

Sherlock Homes and The Shadows of St.Petersburg

"A psychological account of a crime" - that's how Fyodor Dostoyevsky described his novel *Crime and Punishment*, which tells of two horrific ax murders in St. Petersburg. It becomes much more than a mere "account", however, when a pair of dead bodies turn up in London's East End, their heads split open by an axe blade.

To Scotland Yard, the crimes are murders to solve. To Sherlock Holmes, they present an intriguing puzzle. But to the literary man, Dr. John H. Watson, they seem a deliberate restaging of the brutal murders depicted in Dostoyevsky's narrative. If Watson is right, what can be the purpose behind an actual recreation of the fictional killings?

Blocking the answer to that question is a mysterious assortment of English and Russian eccentrics, and one can only wonder if the startling revelation at the end will be dramatic enough to set matters straight.

Also from MX Publishing

When the papal apartments are burgled in 1901, Sherlock Holmes is summoned to Rome by Pope Leo XII. After learning from the pontiff that several priceless cameos that could prove compromising to the church, and perhaps determine the future of the newly unified Italy, have been stolen, Holmes is asked to recover them. In a parallel story, Michelangelo, the toast of Rome in 1501 after the unveiling of his Pieta, is commissioned by Pope Alexander VI, the last of the Borgia pontiffs, with creating the cameos that will bedevil Holmes and the papacy four centuries later. For fans of Conan Doyle's immortal detective, the game is always afoot. However, the great detective has never encountered an adversary quite like the one with whom he crosses swords in "The Vatican Cameos.."

"An extravagantly imagined and beautifully written Holmes story"

(**Lee Child**, NY Times Bestselling author,
Jack Reacher series)

Also from MX Publishing

Our bestselling books are our short story collections;

'Lost Stories of Sherlock Holmes' , 'The Outstanding Mysteries
of Sherlock Holmes', The Papers of Sherlock Holmes Volume 1
and 2, 'Untold Adventures of Sherlock Holmes' (and the sequel
'Studies in Legacy) and 'Sherlock Holmes in Pursuit', 'The
Cotswold Werewolf and Other Stories of Sherlock Holmes' –
and many more......

Also from MX Publishing

"Phil Growick's, 'The Secret Journal of Dr Watson', is an adventure which takes place in the latter part of Holmes and Watson's lives. They are entrusted by HM Government (although not officially) and the King no less to undertake a rescue mission to save the Romanovs, Russia's Royal family from a grisly end at the hand of the Bolsheviks. There is a wealth of detail in the story but not so much as would detract us from the enjoyment of the story. Espionage, counter-espionage, the ace of spies himself, double-agents, double-crossers...all these flit across the pages in a realistic and exciting way. All the characters are extremely well-drawn and Mr Growick, most importantly, does not falter with a very good ear for Holmesian dialogue indeed. Highly recommended. A five-star effort."
The Baker Street Society

Also from MX Publishing

The Missing Authors Series

Sherlock Holmes and The Adventure of The Grinning Cat
Sherlock Holmes and The Nautilus Adventure
Sherlock Holmes and The Round Table Adventure

"Joseph Svec, III is brilliant in entwining two endearing and enduring classics of literature, blending the factual with the fantastical; the playful with the pensive; and the mischievous with the mysterious. We shall, all of us young and old, benefit with a cup of tea, a tranquil afternoon, and a copy of Sherlock Holmes, The Adventure of the Grinning Cat."
Amador County Holmes Hounds Sherlockian Society

Also from MX Publishing

The Detective and The Woman Series

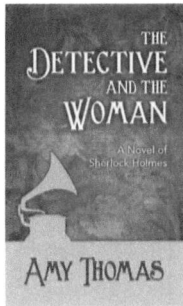 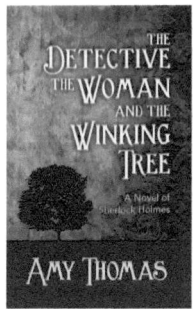 

The Detective and The Woman
The Detective, The Woman and The Winking Tree
The Detective, The Woman and The Silent Hive

"The book is entertaining, puzzling and a lot of fun. I believe the author has hit on the only type of long-term relationship possible for Sherlock Holmes and Irene Adler. The details of the narrative only add force to the romantic defects we expect in both of them and their growth and development are truly marvelous to watch. This is not a love story. Instead, it is a coming-of-age tale starring two of our favorite characters."
Philip K Jones

Also from MX Publishing

During the elaborate funeral for Queen Victoria, a group of Irish separatists breaks into Westminster Abbey and steals the Coronation Stone, on which every monarch of England has been crowned since the 14th century. After learning of the theft from Mycroft, Sherlock Holmes is tasked with recovering the stone and returning it to England. In pursuit of the many-named stone, which has a rich and colorful history, Holmes and Watson travel to Ireland in disguise as they try to infiltrate the Irish Republican Brotherhood, the group they believe responsible for the theft. The story features a number of historical characters, including a very young Michael Collins, who would go on to play a prominent role in Irish history; John Theodore Tussaud, the grandson of Madame Tussaud; and George Bradley, the dean of Westminster at the time of the theft. There are also references to a number of other Victorian luminaries, including Joseph Lister and Frederick Treves.